It Girl

Hollywood to Olympus, Book 4

Elle Rush

Published 2016

Cover design by Lyn Taylor
Formatted by Self-Publishing Services LLC.
(www.Self-Publishing-Service.com)

Blurb

Caitlin's television career is taking off, thanks in part to her chemistry with her co-star. Sean wants to move their romance off-screen, but his stalker has other ideas. Can they find a balance or will their fame rip them apart?

Dedication

To my family, with much love as always. My mom, who gave me her love of reading; my dad, who brought home books by the bag; and my sister, who told me to go for it when I said I wanted to create my own stories.

Acknowledgements

Thanks to Holli and Drew for their constant encouragement and my chat room girls for getting me through the rough spots and the I-donwannas.

Chapter 1

SEAN Glenn bolted out of the fire door, hiked his gleaming white toga above his knees, and sprinted hell-for-leather down the narrow street separating the Olympus soundstage from the neighboring building. He blew past a trolley carrying a load of passengers who had paid for a behind-the-scenes studio tour, and waved at the tourists. "Sorry, can't stop. Gotta run!"

He heard a couple people say, "Hey, that was Eros," before the sound of a heavy metal door clanking against the wall echoed down the passage. Sean slowed slightly and brushed a lock of red hair out of his eyes as he chanced a look over his shoulder. Damn, Dionysus was fast.

A tall black man in a pink toga stood in the doorway and pointed at him. "You're a dead man, Glenn." Sean expected Mike Mosley to be a little perturbed about his new costume. What he'd forgotten about Mike was that the man was faster than he looked. Sean had been a state-champion basketball player back in college. Mike had run track.

Sean made it to the corner before he caught a glimpse of his second victim. Caitlin Kelly, who played his love interest Psyche on the show, looked ready to kill him.

It had been a little more than a year since the first time Sean laid eyes on Caitlin. He and some friends were watching a charity volleyball match when she walked onto the court and caught his eye. Sean had promptly been warned off by Caitlin's pseudo-big brother, as well as by his own friends. For her part, his playboy history had immediately put him out of the running for the good girl.

There was no doubt she was gorgeous; every man in the stands hoped she was as hot as her dark, sultry looks promised. Sean didn't think about her brain until he learned she'd been struggling for a break in show business for the better part of a decade. It took strength and determination not to quit in this business. Caitlin's stubbornness in going after what she wanted only made her more attractive to him.

Sean was thrilled to have another shot with her a few weeks later when Caitlin appeared on the set of Olympus in a limited three-episode appearance. Even better, she'd been cast as his character's love interest, and he got to spend nearly a month working with her. Unfortunately, she didn't seem to return his infatuation. Halfway into the show's break between seasons three and four, the studio announced that Caitlin would be returning. Sean had used the time to come up with a new plan of attack. This stunt was his opening move to get her attention.

He stumbled when the sunlight hit her black hair, giving her a halo effect. She looked stunning in cotton-candy pink, and the incredible vision of her meant Sean couldn't regret the prank, no matter how risky it was. That didn't mean he was stupid enough to hang around. When he heard Caitlin shout, "Get him, Mike!" he took off again and headed for the soundstage's main doors on the other side of the building. His co-conspirators were supposed to be ready to spring part two of their welcome.

Sean loved his job. He had never intended to get into show business. He considered it to be a fortunate life detour. His plan in college was to get into coaching, preferably basketball or another sport at any level. He'd needed the drama credit for his degree, which had led to a couple local commercials, which had later turned into a handful of national commercials, and a move out to Los Angeles from Wyoming. He did a few guest appearances and suddenly he was Eros, the Greek god of love. Nobody expected a cable drama like Olympus to hit as big as it did. Sean was stunned they'd made it to their fourth season. Now he got to do stuff like this and get paid for it.

Maybe not like this, exactly. He, Chris Peck and Nick Thurston, Zeus and Ares respectively, caused most of the trouble on set. Fortunately for the rest of the cast, they went after each other more often than they targeted anyone else. Today was special; they were initiating the two most recent additions to the cast. He had set up the joke. Everybody else was waiting for him at the main entrance for the punch line.

The entire cast and crew burst into applause as Mike and Caitlin caught him. "Welcome to Olympus! Watch your backs."

Mike shook his fist good-naturedly at them. "Can I have my real wardrobe now? This is not my color," he said.

Caitlin's response shocked him to silence. She gave hugs to everybody, whatever she whispered into their ears making each of them smile or laugh. She left him for last.

She was a good six inches shorter than him, but she was taller than he expected. He glanced down and saw she'd made her sprint in sandals with two-inch heels, putting her at 5'10". Her shoulder length black hair was wild after her run; the strands stuck to her face highlighted her cheekbones. The ruby-red lipstick she wore guaranteed he was paying attention to her lips when she grabbed his shoulders and pulled him down for a fast, hard kiss on his mouth. "Game on, cowboy," she said.

* * * *

She'd been expecting something. After the stories her friend Sydney Richardson had shared about her boyfriend Chris's pranks on the set, Caitlin Kelly knew she wouldn't get away unscathed. Truth be told, she was impressed. The toga stunt was a pretty good joke.

She and Mike Mosley had both had guest roles on Olympus in previous years, but they were starting as permanent members this season. She'd been on guard at the table read where they went over the script for the first episode. Sean, Chris, Nick, and the rest of them had been utterly professional. They'd lulled her into a false sense of security. Then her wardrobe arrived and she was certain something was up.

She took the outfit to the trailer beside hers and knocked on the door. "What on earth is this?" she asked Glinda Crawford, who played Aphrodite.

The blonde opened the door to invite her in, dressed in her own pink toga. "Aren't they hideous?" Glinda replied with a laugh.

"What was wrong with good old white?" Caitlin asked.

"Apparently they're tired of having to deal with the color problem in post-production editing. I heard the material they used for the togas last year didn't come out well on camera so they want to try this instead."

Granted, while Glinda's explanation had sounded weird, it wasn't completely unbelievable. Depending on lighting and other factors, blue could look white on screen, purple showed up as red, and green turned invisible.

Besides, the two of them weren't the only ones with the new wardrobe. Caitlin turned when Glinda waved out the window to Chris, who was holding a similar outfit at arm's length. She couldn't hear him, but it looked like he was cursing up a storm. "I guess I'd better get changed then. We're due on set in ten minutes," Caitlin said.

"I need to finish getting ready too. See you there."

Glinda smiled when she kicked her out. Caitlin thought nothing of it since the actress was always smiling. Caitlin buttoned herself into the costume and headed to the soundstage. She ran into Mike on the way. They snickered when they saw each other. She and Mike ignored the stares from the crew as they walked in. They had no idea they'd been thoroughly punked until they arrived at the set of Olympus's banquet hall and found the rest of the cast decked out in regular white togas.

Sean stepped forward. Caitlin should have known. His reputation as a prankster was only beaten by his history as a ladies' man. It was a shame because he was a good-looking man. Caitlin couldn't understand why some women dismissed gingers; redheads were sexy as hell, even if one of them did set her up as part of a public spectacle. "Did you guys fall into a vat of Pepto Bismol or what?" he asked, not even trying to keep a straight face.

And that's, as they say, when the fight started.

Chapter 2

IT might have been a first. They'd finished their first day of filming on time. Sean jogged a few steps to catch Caitlin, who was on her way to her trailer. "You okay?" he asked. Between takes she'd been quieter than normal. Unfortunately, he couldn't come out and say that. He didn't want her to know how closely he'd paid attention during the three episodes she'd filmed with him the previous season.

"I'm fine," she said.

"You aren't upset about the toga thing, are you?" He'd been trying to get a date with Caitlin for weeks. Months. He hated to think his chances dropped from slim to none because she didn't have a sense of humor.

Caitlin stopped in her tracks. "No! Not at all. That was funny as hell. I can't believe you went so far as to involve Glinda and Chris. Their pink togas sold the deal. It was a great joke. I loved it. It made me feel like I was really one of the team. Thanks for including me."

"You're welcome," Sean said, relief flooding him. "I knew you and Mike would think it was funny. Eventually."

"You didn't actually dye any costumes, did you?" Caitlin asked. "My mom worked at a dry-cleaners at one of my dad's postings. I'm telling you now; those togas will never be white again."

She was too cute. "Don't worry about it. We had them specially made when we found out you were coming aboard."

"Exactly how long have you been sitting on this?"

"Since August." Five months sounded like a long lead time for a practical joke, but Sean had pulled more elaborate pranks in his day.

"You do know I'm going to get even, right?" she bluffed. She looked as threatening as a kitten. A sexy kitten. "I hear Mike is threatening more vengeance than me." Sean couldn't take her seriously, not when she gave him that grin of hers, the one so big it crinkled the corners of her eyes. It hit him like a lightning bolt to his groin.

"I think I can take you."

"You're not ready for me, cowboy."

That was an opening if he ever heard one. "We need to celebrate your first day as a full-time series regular. Let me take you out for a drink." He'd asked her before; his persistence had to pay off eventually.

Caitlin paused at her trailer door. "I'm busy tonight."

"How is it you're always busy when I ask you out? Are you seeing somebody?" He hoped not. Sean figured he would have heard something with all the time he spent hanging around Chris and Sydney, and Nick and Ashleigh. The guys' significant others were good friends of Caitlin's. If anyone knew, they would. Despite trying to play it cool, his friends knew something was going on with him and Caitlin. They simply didn't realize the "something" was in the pursuit stages.

"Have you considered asking me what I'm doing instead of getting your exercise jumping to conclusions?"

He'd thought about it. He hadn't followed through. Layla was going to kick his ass.

Layla Andrews, the show's Hera, had told him months ago how to approach Caitlin. He'd shrugged off her recommended advice. Caitlin's latest question made him wonder if he'd wasted those weeks for nothing.

"We're wrapped for the day. What are you doing tonight?" he asked dutifully.

"Me? I'm going to work."

Caitlin had given him that answer more than once. He'd always assumed she was giving him a gentle brush-off. This time he finally paid attention and was shocked to realize she wasn't lying. Her smirk told him so. He didn't have the chance to follow up because of the blonde who materialized beside him.

"Hi, Martine. And friend," Sean said to Olympus's PR guru. Martine Peeples had warned him she'd be escorting various reporters around the lot for a few days. She was attempting to boost the show's profile. Six months after season three's finale, a new crop of series dominated the airwaves. Olympus would have to fight to maintain its spot at the top of the heap.

"Sean, I'd like to introduce Jared Parker. He's part of the visiting Australian media group. Jared, this is Sean Glenn. He plays Eros on the show."

Sean offered his hand. "Nice to meet you." He didn't mind taking his turn charming the press. It was part of the job.

The Aussie had a good grip. "Thanks. I saw you when you were playing for the Cowboys," Jared said.

"How did you end up at a University of Wyoming b-ball game?"

"I did a semester in Denver. Journalism. You trounced them."

Martine interrupted before they got too deep into basketball talk. "Jared is talking to several members of the cast today. If you could answer his questions and give me a buzz once you're finished, I've arranged for him to speak to Layla next."

"No problem," Sean said. "I'll call you when we're done."

They talked college sports for almost ten minutes before the reporter shifted the conversation to actual interview questions.

"What's it like to film a series in togas?" Jared started.

"Drafty. Very drafty. I have a new respect for actors who are stuck in kilts for weeks on end when they film period pieces in Scotland."

"What's been the most fun you've had on set to date?"

"In front of the camera? Last year's food-fight. Originally, the scene was just supposed to be a glass of wine in the face. I'm very glad Layla suggested we throw caution to the wind, and throw everything else we grab from the banquet hall table. It was epic. Our togas had to be retired." The scene he'd had with Layla had turned into the stuff of legend.

"I hear this is a fun place to work. Who's the biggest prankster on set?"

"Me."

"Besides you?"

"Chris Peck. I'd like to elaborate but I've been threatened with a slow and painful death if I implicate him in any way regarding the incident that left Nick Thurston locked out of his trailer wearing nothing but a towel and a smile," Sean said. That should be enough to keep things interesting for a while. In addition to that stunt, Chris had also not only organized Russ's never-again-to-be-mentioned birthday clown-o-gram incident, but he'd also managed to set Sean up to take the fall. Sean was yet to match that.

"As Eros, can you actually shoot a bow and arrow?"

"I'm learning. I'm not a great archer. Thankfully most of those scenes are me drawing back the bow, followed by a close-up of an arrow sticking out of what Eros was supposed to hit."

Jared frowned a little at that news. "That's disappointing. I thought your fight scenes were supposed to be authentic."

"The fight scenes don't use projectiles. Our hand-to-hand combat scenes are completely authentic. No special effects. We've had some great fight coordinators. Between us and our stunt-doubles, we do all the sword-fighting in front of the camera. If you're around for the next one, you should come and watch," he said. The weapons weren't solid steel, but swinging a light-weight broadsword still took effort. Sean was wiped after training days.

"You now have an on-screen love interest. How do you like working with Caitlin Kelly?"

"She's great. Very talented. I look forward to working with her more this season."

"Do you have an off-screen love interest?"

"Not presently." He didn't add he was working on it.

"Did you work on any projects during hiatus?" Jared asked.

"No, I'm bit more of a slacker than some of my cast-mates. I did do…" Sean let his voice trail off as he counted in his head. "…four different fan conventions and events. Those were a blast. I've been doing fan-cons since the first season and I always have a great time. I think Olympus's fans are the best ones out there. " He'd been friendly to the largely female audience, but he hadn't been as flirtatious as he had in past seasons. Not with Caitlin on his mind.

"Would you do another one?"

Sean grinned. "In a heartbeat."

A few more questions finished off the interview and Sean delivered the reporter to Layla's trailer. He stopped by Caitlin's, but she was gone. To work, or so she said.

He had no idea what work she was referring to, but he was going to find out.

* * * *

Caitlin eyed the coffee machine like it offered a Schedule 1 narcotic hit. She needed it badly, although she knew she should simply walk away from the pot. At this point the caffeine would do more long-term harm than immediate good. She was tired. So very tired.

She wasn't complaining. It had taken her a decade to get to the point where people wanted to hire her to do anything. Now she was working full-time as an actress, and she was putting in almost as many hours on her musical career. After years of crappy part-time jobs, the income and stability was like a dream. She finally had a real career. Two of them.

Murder victim, waitress, stewardess, bimbo girlfriend—she'd played them all. She'd even had a name and lines in her last two roles. Six months ago, out of the blue, her agent got a call from Blue Note Productions asking her to audition for a minor role in Three Date Rule, the romantic comedy starring Savannah Graves and Caitlin's current co-star, Chris Peck.

Caitlin couldn't prove her friend's boyfriend had recommended her for the part, although it was a pretty good guess. She wouldn't have held it against him if he had. Caitlin wasn't above walking through doors others had opened for her. Chris also swore he had nothing to do with her getting the role as Psyche on Olympus. It was nice to know she got her biggest role to date on her own merits.

On the other hand, there was Charlie. She'd been playing bass guitar in Charlie Oscar Echo since high school. A bunch of fellow army brats got together and ran the "Class of Oh Eight" through the military alphabet code and ended up with their band's name. For years they'd jammed for fun, or played at the occasional school dance to earn enough to buy themselves new equipment. They'd gone their own ways after graduation—she and Bobby Wheaton left for college, Peter Blackwood went on a walkabout, and Gregory Mills enlisted for a couple tours with the Air Force. A few years later they all found themselves in Los Angeles at the same time. Older, more experienced, and most importantly, broke, they resurrected Charlie and decided to move from a garage band to professional musicians. Whether it was luck or talent, they developed a small following from their paying gigs, and their popularity and paychecks started to increase.

Break, their first full-length album, which they'd recorded over the summer, exceeded everybody's expectations. The video that went with the title song they released went viral in the indie world, and all of a sudden Charlie Oscar Echo was in demand at the same clubs that had previously slammed doors in their faces. Now that everybody wanted them, Caitlin and the guys were trying to figure out how to grab as many pieces of the pie as they could.

As a result, the band paid well, but still not enough for anyone to quit their regular jobs. That meant they had to get creative. Tonight was about fan appreciation. Their first video was top of the line: it showed in the choreography and editing and everything else. It had been their introduction to the masses.

This time they wanted to get to know their new fans,

or at least give that impression, so they were going low tech. It was Caitlin's idea. She used words like "intimate" and "raw." And "cheap." The last one may have been the selling point.

A friend with a handheld camera had offered to shoot the entire video. They had decided on an unplugged sound. They were now set up in the living room of an empty house, a 1950s ranch-style home with an old, red-brick fireplace, and dusty, scratched-up hardwood floors. They sat on crates, wearing jeans and shirts. Camping lanterns and candles lit the room. If it worked as Caitlin envisioned, it was going to be amazing.

Except she was singing to the beat of a different drummer. Literally.

"What are you doing?" Caitlin asked.

"Singing Watching Him Watching Her. What are you doing?" Greg shot back.

"Singing Not Quite Home. Why aren't you?"

The lead singer flinched. "I forgot to text you. We're changing the order of our releases. Peter and I worked a deal and we need the video for Watching Him Watching Her done yesterday. Can you do it?"

The song they wanted to do now was a ballad Greg had written while he was overseas after his fiancée called off their wedding. The girl was gone, but the song lived on. "Of course I can do it. But warn a girl when you do something like this, would you?" Caitlin didn't have a problem making the change, or about not being informed of the deal before it was finalized. She had absolute trust in her boys. Neglecting to keep her in the loop was another matter.

Then she flubbed the bridge into the second verse for the second time.

"Cait-girl, you okay?" Bobby asked.

"I'm fine. Just tired." Like they couldn't tell. She barely got the words out before they were swallowed by a yawn. One day down, another three months of shooting to go.

"I made coffee. There's some left," Peter offered, holding up his thermos.

"God, no! I mean, no thanks," Caitlin backpedaled. Peter shared the Cuban half of her heritage. It showed in his coffee-making skills. "I'm already too caffeinated. Do we have any water?"

Greg tossed her a bottle. "Should we try again tomorrow?"

Caitlin shook her head as she guzzled the ice-cold liquid. "We're not going to get less busy. Give me a minute and we'll try again."

It took more than a minute. She was ready to go when Greg and Peter started goofing around with a song they'd been trying to get right for a month. Eventually they settled into playing Watching Him Watching Her.

"Nailed it!" Bobby did a short drum roll in celebration.

"We did," Caitlin agreed.

"One more time for some different camera angles?" Peter suggested.

The next two runs were equally good. "I can't wait to see what it looks like," Caitlin said. "But I've got to get going. I have an early call time tomorrow."

"Peter and I will work on the editing over the next couple days. We'll let you know when the final version is ready."

It took three trips to load everything into their vehicles, and a few more minutes to tidy the living room so they could leave it the way they'd found it. Bobby folded his long legs into her passenger seat while Caitlin started her gleaming white half-ton. The drummer lived a few blocks from her so she'd offered him a ride home after he caught a ride to the house with Peter.

Bobby rolled down the window and let the cool night air fill the cab. He ran his fingers through his shaggy blond hair and heaved a heavy sigh.

"What's up, Bobby-o?" Caitlin asked as she lifted her thick ponytail off the back of her neck.

"I'm sleepy."

"Me, too," she sympathized.

"That's what worries me. I'm wiped after putting in eight hours behind a desk, and you're doing God knows what for twelve or more hours a day."

"I'm living the dream, baby." She'd spent years working three or more jobs at a time to make ends meet. Working one and a half was nothing, especially since the one paid better than the rest combined. "I'd say I'll sleep when I'm dead, but let's face it, I like my zzz's. I'll do double duty for the next four months, I'll be fine. Besides, by the time I finish filming for the season, we should be ready to record our next album."

"And in the meantime?"

Caitlin took her eyes from the road long enough to give him a good, hard look. "Mine isn't the only schedule we're working around. I made a commitment to you guys. I'm going to keep it. We aren't that busy right now, and I have no guarantee Psyche is going to survive longer than one season on the show. Mortals tend not to do well against crazy Greek gods. Let's cross that bridge when we come to it, shall we?"

Bobby nodded. "Fair enough. I'm just worried about you."

She reached across the gear shift and punched him in the arm. "I know, Bobby-o. I'll be okay. I promise."

Chapter 3

IT didn't take long to fall behind. An extra fifteen minutes to fix some make-up here, a twenty-minute delay to replace a light there, and by the end of the week they were finishing their shooting days at midnight. Sean swung his arms in circles as he took deep breaths of the cool night air in an attempt to wake himself up. If he were lucky, he'd fall face-first into his pillow just after midnight.

Thoughts of pillows led to thoughts of beds, which led to thoughts of Caitlin in bed. Sexy, naked, uninhibited Caitlin. Sleeping, trusting, vulnerable Caitlin. Conversations with Caitlin in the dark, where he could wrap locks of her luscious hair around his fingers while they discussed everything and nothing.

All of a sudden Sean wasn't sleepy anymore. Awake didn't mean paying attention though, he thought, right after he jumped when a tap on his shoulder caught him unaware.

"Hey, Cait," he said, praying his voice didn't squeak after the shock. "What's up?" After she'd turned him down for dinner after their second day of shooting, and said no to a date after the third, he'd backed off to formulate a new plan of attack.

"Did everybody get one of these?" she asked, holding her cell phone.

Sean shook his head to clear it. Caitlin was soft and quiet, two things he'd never seen unless she was in front of a camera and the script called for it. "What is it? Can I see?"

"Check your own email."

He pulled out his phone and found an urgent email from Martine. He scanned through the message and stumbled when he got to the details. "Is this right?" Sean looked up with a huge smile on his face. "So you're one of the tributes? I mean, volunteers? That's great! These events aren't terrible. Except for the chicken. It's always chicken." That wasn't precisely true. Anywhere else in the country a fundraising dinner meant chicken. In LA there were a disturbing amount of plates that were vegan instead of actual meat. For a Wyoming boy like him, the huge number of steak-free zones in the city was pretty terrifying.

"Sean, keep reading."

He returned to the email, nodding as he hit the points he knew about. Yes, there was a charity dinner next week. Yes, the network expected some members of Olympus to attend. Yes, they were supposed to make the rounds and be seen. He kept reading and found the line about him and Caitlin introducing one of the guests of honor. "Hey, we finally get to go out on a date."

"It's not a date. It's work."

"It could be a date." He sure as hell wasn't going to get one with her any other way at his current pace. "We could make it a date if we wanted to." The memory of Caitlin's lecture earlier in the week about asking her out instead of making assumptions flashed a warning light in his head. "Would you like to treat this work function as a real date and go to the banquet with me?"

He waited for a yes. Then he waited for a no. Then he waited for any kind of response at all. "Caitlin?"

"You're very handsome," she said from out of nowhere.

That wasn't an answer. "Thank you?" Sean had no idea where was she going with this line of conversation.

"And you're funny."

"Okay." Compliments were good. She wasn't saying anything he didn't want to hear.

"So I like you," she said.

"Is that good?" Sean asked.

"It's not bad. I usually like the guys I date."

"I can see that being helpful. I like you too," Sean said. Caitlin was being quiet again. It made him nervous.

"I also usually don't date players," she added, "and you are most definitely a player."

Sean was fucked. Not in the way he wanted to be, either. He couldn't deny it because his reputation went beyond the tabloids. He'd had fun as the god of love, and his conquests were numerous and well publicized. Everybody knew it. He hadn't been serious with any of the women he'd dated, and he'd been careful to make sure they knew that going in. Unfortunately for him, Caitlin had been upfront from their first meeting about being the commitment type. He hadn't stood a chance.

His hook-ups dropped off substantially after he filmed his first episode with Caitlin the previous summer. He hadn't noticed he'd subconsciously removed himself from the dating scene until he'd run into Mike in October. They'd been having a drink to celebrate Mike's new permanent role when he'd asked whom Sean had been seeing. Sean realized that not only did he not have an answer; he hadn't had one for some time. His little brain had made the decision to go after Caitlin before his big brain realized it. Now he was playing catch-up.

"I do have a history," he admitted. "But if you'll think about it, I haven't done anything to add to that lately. There's a very good reason for that."

"What reason?"

Sean thought about his answer. He waited until she looked at him and met his eye. "Ask me again in a month," he said. He figured the, I've-changed-and-it's-all-for-you truth would scare her more than his reputation, which had already done enough damage to their potential—and at the moment, fictional—relationship.

As it was, his answer seemed to surprise her. At least, that's how he took the raised eyebrow, smile, and full-body once-over she gave him. It only lasted a moment, but for that one second he had her.

"I will," she said.

"You didn't answer my question. Would you like to turn this work date into a real date?"

"It won't be a real date."

"Go with me anyway. Please."

"Okay," she said. "Let's give this a try."

Finally.

* * * *

"I think I made a big mistake." Caitlin twisted in front of the mirror and studied the ensemble she intended to wear to the network charity dinner in two nights' time. The turquoise cocktail dress fit her like a second skin, promising everything without actually revealing much. The outfit wasn't new; she'd bought it for a Charlie Oscar Echo concert the year before and her thrifty heart was happy for the chance to wear it again. She might be on a hit television show, but it didn't mean her paycheck matched yet. She had to start making friends and influencing people quickly if she was going to be making more personal appearances. She needed the swag.

Ashleigh Jessup, friend, fellow dancer, and landlord, whistled and twirled her finger as an order for Caitlin to spin and give her audience a 360-degree view. "No, there is absolutely nothing wrong with you," Ashleigh said. "You look gorgeous."

Sydney Richardson, friend, fellow volleyball player, and owner of the strappy heels she was borrowing, twirled her finger in the other direction and Caitlin obliged her with another turn. "Ash is right. You look perfect. Dammit. I wish I could wear that color."

"It's not the dress. It's Sean," Caitlin said. "I shouldn't have said yes."

"Why not?" Ashleigh asked.

"Because he's a horn-dog who goes after anything in a skirt. He caught me in a moment of weakness."

"He was wearing his toga, wasn't he?" Sydney asked, as if she knew the answer.

"Yes," Caitlin admitted slowly, although she hadn't thought about it at the time.

"It's always the toga," Ashleigh said. "They're like Kryptonite to women. We see the thighs and the chest and the arms—"

"Oh, the arms," Sydney interrupted with a sigh.

"—and our brains shut down," Ashleigh finished. "I think they know and use the togas against us."

If anyone would know about the toga power the gods of Olympus wielded, her friends would. A little over a year ago, Chris Peck volunteered to act as the grand prize in the show's online fan appreciation contest. Sydney won him as her slave for a day. Despite a little stumbling in the beginning, they'd obviously enjoyed their time together, because the pair had been inseparable ever since.

Ashleigh was dating another Olympic god, Nick Thurston; Sydney had gotten them together too. Nick had needed a dance instructor for a theater role he took during the break between seasons and he'd fallen hard for the gorgeous blonde. Their path had a rockier start, which, after a rough few months, seemed to be headed into smoother waters.

Of course the contest's biggest winner—non-romantically speaking—had been Caitlin herself. A few months after meeting the actors through Sydney, she'd been cast for three episodes as Psyche, Sean's on-screen love interest. After the characters had become fan favorites from their very first scene, the producers brought her back as a full cast member for the current season. The problem was that the characters weren't the only ones attracted to each other. Caitlin had been putting Sean off for months with legitimate excuses. Now she'd run out of reasons not to go out with him. Reasons and will.

"You are the ones who told me I need to stop dating Mr. Right Now and think about having a real relationship. I don't think a quick fling with a self-admitted one-night-stand king qualifies." Caitlin wouldn't say she was commitment-phobic; she simply had very high standards—standards that included a man who understood she wasn't going to sacrifice her career for him like her mother had done for her dad. Unsurprisingly, her short-term boyfriends weren't concerned about this qualification. Also unsurprisingly, the ones who lasted beyond her usual one-month burn-out period got pissed off when they discovered they weren't the exception to her rule and didn't make it to month three. A guy who truly understood was impossible to find.

"First of all, it's not a fling. It's barely a date. You haven't committed yourself 'til death do you part. Secondly, you aren't going to be alone with him. It's going to be you, Sean, a dozen of your co-workers, and two hundred complete strangers. Thirdly, you have to make a presentation in the middle of it. It's not like you're going to have a chance to get horizontal with him. And fourthly, he is smokin' hot, which is never a bad thing. You're allowed to have a little fun. He's not as hot as Chris, but he'll do," Sydney lectured from the sofa.

"He's everything you've been telling me to stay away from," Caitlin protested.

Sydney bit her lip. "Technically, yes. But you said he's working on cleaning up his act. If things go well and you like him, you can re-evaluate and think about a real date next time."

The redhead knew something. Caitlin was sure of it. Sydney was the poster-child of responsibility and would never lead her astray. Unfortunately she was also the poster-child of discretion and she wasn't going to give her any more hints if she didn't want to. "Why aren't you going to this shindig with Chris? We could have gone together," Caitlin asked, changing the subject.

"Because I don't work for the studio. I also may have bribed him to say I was unavailable. I went to that awards show with him last month. That was more than enough for a while," Sydney explained. Sydney's lack of desire to be in the spotlight and Chris's professional requirement to be there was their sole incompatibility. Syd didn't say much about it, but Caitlin knew they had worked hard to find a balance they could both live with.

Ashleigh shrugged before Caitlin could pose the same question to her. "Nick's taking his mother since she's in the network's new crime drama. I'm not going to be a third wheel to that pair."

"So you're both abandoning me. Thanks a bunch. After everything I've done for you."

"We promise to be awake when you call us with an after-event report," Ashleigh said. Sydney crossed her heart in agreement.

"Fine. Like you said, nothing's going to happen. It's not a date."

Chapter 4

WERE flowers necessary? Sean didn't know if anybody sent their dates flowers anymore, but traditionally, flowers had been a thing once. Hadn't they? Caitlin seemed like the traditional date sort. What if she expected some? He couldn't call either of his baby sisters because they'd give him the wrong answer just to mess with him. His mom would have too many questions.

This was going to be a disaster.

Luckily for him, he had another source. He pulled out his phone and punched in a number that had steadily made its way up his "most dialed" list over the last few months. "Hi. Are you busy?" he asked.

"No, come on over."

He knocked on the door and pulled it open when he heard the "enter." He stopped dead halfway through it. A fat vase full of white lilies sat squarely in the middle of Layla Andrews's coffee table. A smaller bouquet of pink tulips on the counter caught his eyes next. Apparently, flowers in general were still a thing. Good to know.

"What's up, Sean? Are you worried about tomorrow's scenes?"

Because he hadn't taken the traditional route into an acting career, Sean knew his training was lacking. He pretty much lucked his way through the initial two seasons, first with limited screen time, then with bravado. He knew he couldn't continue that way, so he quietly took acting lessons. Olympus's third season thrust Eros into the spotlight and he'd been forced to ask for help from all quarters. Surprisingly, Layla turned out to be his best tutor. The show's resident ice queen recently thawed into a surprisingly tolerable co-star after two years of anti-social behavior. She'd burned a few bridges among the other actors during that time, although she was slowly making amends. Now Sean liked to think he was one of her closest friends on set. They helped each other out: her with his acting, and him with her relationships with their co-stars.

What he was about to ask her was beyond the scope of their existing friendship. They weren't that close, but he was out of time and out of options. "What do you think of flowers on first dates?" he blurted out.

"For me or in general?" She studied his face for a second, and nodded. "Oh, for Caitlin. I don't think that's a good idea."

"The flowers or Caitlin?" Because he was only willing to give up the flowers and, technically, he didn't even have Caitlin yet.

"Caitlin."

"Why would she be a bad idea?"

"Workplace romances are risky. Doubly so in this industry," Layla warned.

"Says the woman who's dating our former fight coordinator."

She laughed. "That is true. You'll note Russ is no longer working here though. I've seen far too many actors fall in love alongside their characters. The affair usually lasts less than a year after the project ends. You've heard the stories."

"I'm willing to risk it," Sean said. "I can't worry about something that might happen two years from now. First things first. What does a guy do on a first date when he's out to impress?"

Layla was one of the few people who knew how long he'd been serious about Caitlin. The guys had guessed over the summer, but Layla had been trying to guide him for almost a year. He should have started listening to her earlier. She looked at him sadly. "The dinner isn't going to be your first date with Caitlin."

"Of course it is. We've never gone out before and tomorrow we are."

Layla shook her head. "You're going to a work thing together. It doesn't count as a date."

"Well, I'm counting it as a date. The best first date in the history of first dates." Sean didn't think he was being unreasonably optimistic. Any time he got to spend with Caitlin would be amazing.

* * * *

Twenty-eight hours later, things were going well. Better than he expected. Between his tuxedo, a fresh haircut, and a straight-razor shave that morning, he was red-carpet ready. He'd even bribed Nick to get Caitlin's address from Ashleigh so he could send her a dozen red roses. Layla had said that while corsages were out, flowers were always in. Sean had it in hand. Until he saw her.

Caitlin came through her apartment block door just as he pressed her suite's buzzer. She was primped and polished and bound in a little blue number that had him drooling. Her swept-up black hair revealed her neck, and her long dangling earrings brushed her uncovered shoulders. All that bare skin almost drove him to his knees.

She'd also done some smoky makeup around her eyes and Sean was certain the deep brown pools of light were looking straight through him. He faked a cough to give him an excuse to touch the corners of his mouth.

Surprisingly, his tongue wasn't actually hanging out of his mouth.

"You look incredible," he choked out. Why had he insisted they go out on their first date? He should have planned to spend it in bed. "Are you ready to go?" He needed them to get moving. If he didn't, they were never getting out of there.

He was a little disappointed when Caitlin spent the ride reviewing their introduction speech rather than talking. Once they had it down cold, she relaxed.

"Ashleigh says I should ask you to ask me to dance if the opportunity arises," she said.

This was his cross-roads. Did he want to keep it work-friendly or did he want to see if they were on a date? "Do you think you can keep up?"

Caitlin smiled at him, and he knew she was full-on flirting by the matching glint in her eye. "I think I can hold my own with you."

* * * *

Stop it, Caitlin. Stop it right now. She never did take instruction well. It wasn't her fault. She couldn't help flirting. Sean was too…everything tonight. Too handsome. Too funny. Too attentive. It was throwing her off-balance.

"Sean, Caitlin, over here, please."

A gentle touch on her waist turned her toward the voice, and she leaned a little closer to Sean. Heat from his hand flooded through her and she glanced at him before she faced the first camera in a long line of photographers. To her surprise, he was peeking down at her at the same time. Getting caught looking was ridiculous enough to send them both into peals of laughter.

A flurry of flashes caught the moment and the paparazzi moved on to another group of people. Actors, producers, executives and other industry bigwigs filled the ballroom. Officially, the network's Giving Back Foundation Dinner was to make annual donations to various charities. Caitlin recognized the night for what it was: a chance to be seen, make connections, and advance careers.

She wasn't opposed. It was part of the gig. She knew most the faces she recognized either had their own charitable foundations or supported causes that were near and dear to their hearts. Caitlin herself was split between Sydney's Curse the Darkness Foundation and a children of fallen soldiers' fund through Charlie Oscar Echo. As long as the money got to where it needed to go, she was fine to go with the flow.

Sean excused himself for a group shot of the boys of Olympus: Chris, Nick, Mike, Jason Ricker—the Canadian who played Hephaestus, and himself. While they clowned around in front of the camera, Caitlin found herself pulled into a cluster of reporters.

"Hi, Jared, nice to meet you. I've heard good things," she said as they finished introductions.

"So have I. I must tell you, I'm half in love with Break. Every song on it. Charlie Oscar Echo has an incredible sound," the Australian journalist said.

Caitlin blinked at the change of subject. "Thank you."

"You sound surprised."

"I am. Not many people know about my involvement with Charlie. Especially here. I could probably count the number of people in the room who have heard of the band, mostly because I'm friends with them all."

"You'd be surprised. I'm shocked there hasn't been more of a crossover with your Olympus fan base."

"I have an Olympus fan base?" It was official. She

liked this guy. If the accent and the fact he conversed with her face and not her chest weren't enough, he knew her music, he liked it, and he liked her acting.

Jared's laughter spread to the other reporters and Caitlin fought the flush that threatened to spread up her neck. Instead she bit the inside of her cheek and whistled a few notes, looking at the ceiling innocently.

"I knew you'd be close to the trouble." Sean's breath was warm in her ear. Although his voice was loud enough to carry to the men, he kept it light and friendly. The powerful arm around her shoulders was less so. The grip he had on her smacked of propriety.

She didn't mind a guy being a little possessive. It felt good to be wanted. Unfortunately for him, Sean hadn't earned that yet.

"What are we laughing about?" Sean asked.

Caitlin shot a pleading look at the reporters. She knew as she did it that she would have to tolerate the teasing they were about to unleash.

"We were discussing the fact Caitlin has half as many fans after three episodes as you have after three years," Jared said.

"I do?" Caitlin said.

"Is she at half? I knew she was catching up," Sean said.

"It won't be long until she pulls ahead."

Sean laughed. "Trust me. I know. I'm keeping my eye on this one."

Caitlin pulled away to look him in the eye. "Are you serious?"

"Please. Once this season airs, we'll be beating them off with a stick. Fans love us," Sean said, giving her a small squeeze.

Get a damn grip on your ego and quit acting like a

damn rookie, Caitlin. This was not the place for squealing over successes. She should be acting like she expected it. She turned back to Jared and shrugged nonchalantly. "What's not to love?"

"Indeed. Caitlin, lovely to see you again. Gentlemen." The new voice belonged to Robert Clancy. She didn't need to introduce him. Everyone already knew the silver-haired fox was one of the biggest producers in town. Caitlin couldn't believe he remembered her name. They'd met once, during one of her four days on the set of Three Date Rule, the movie his company had filmed over the summer.

"I'm sorry to pull her away. I came over because Martine says it's almost time," Sean said to the group. Caitlin looked across the room and saw the show's blonde PR maven with her taller, blonder girlfriend Paris Temple talking with a bunch of actors from SWAT Boyz. As they walked away, Sean slipped his hand into hers and whispered in her ear again. "It's actually not time, but there's no way we are getting a straight shot through the room without having to stop. I wanted a moment alone with you while I could get it."

A moment was all they got before a stacked brunette in black attempted to hip-check Caitlin into a table. Out of reflex rather than intent, Caitlin grabbed the bumper by the arm and used momentum to right herself, spinning the other woman in the other direction.

"You bitch! Get your hands off Eros! I love him!" The bitch in black returned swinging, her fingers clawed to rake her nails across Caitlin's the face.

Caitlin was embarrassed for her. She caught the woman's hand and twisted it with a wrist lock. Her would-be attacker bent at the waist to ease the pressure on her arm. "Let me go! Let me go, you cunt! Eros, help me!" The woman's screams increased. Caitlin tightened her grip. She had a tiger by the tail and wasn't about to let go.

"A little help?" she said to Sean, who was staring at her in morbid delight.

He shook off his shock and beckoned two security guards over to them. "Can you please escort this woman from the premises?" he requested.

Once Caitlin was certain they had her, she released the woman's hand and stepped back. She tugged on the hem of her dress and readjusted the bust as unobtrusively as she could. "We should get over to Martine. She looks like she's about to have a cow," Caitlin said.

Sean put his hand on the small of her back, lower than a friend would, as he steered her in the right direction. Then, suddenly, his hand was gone. Caitlin looked over her shoulder and saw the woman in black was back, and had her tongue stuck down Sean's throat. Sean's hands fluttered for a moment, then gripped the woman's biceps tightly and pushed her away without letting her fall.

"Sorry, she got away from us," the first security guard said.

"Do you need assistance?" Caitlin asked. Her tone sounded friendly, but the guard who was looking at her flinched when he saw her face. If they couldn't do the job, she would, and she made certain they knew it.

"No, thank you. We've got it. I'm sorry, Mr. Glenn, Ms. Kelly. It won't happen again." People politely ignored the woman's flailing and shouting as she was restrained and led away.

Caitlin wanted to check Sean out to make sure the woman hadn't hurt him. He was standing stiffly, with an obviously strained smile on his face. Then he handed

Caitlin off to Martine and Paris. "Excuse me. I need a minute," he choked out before he stalked out of the room.

Caitlin fumed when she saw two suited men with badges pull Sean to the side after he stepped out of the men's room, only Martine's presence blocking the door and Paris's hand on her arm held her still. Caitlin didn't know if she wanted to chase after Sean to make sure he was okay, or go after the deranged fan and ensure she'd never do anything like that again. If a man had put his hands on her like that, she could press sexual assault charges and make them stick. Since it was a woman going after a man who was bigger than her, Sean would be laughed at if he tried. And it was exactly the same thing. Her rage grew.

"I'm going to—" she began.

"Whoa, Caitlin, how about you put those ninja skills back under wraps? There will be no maiming here tonight," Paris cracked, trying to break the tension.

"You know if a male fan did that to me—" Caitlin growled.

"You apparently would have flattened the bastard with very little effort, and rightly so," Martine agreed. "I'll talk to Sean to make sure this is handled properly. I promise. Right now, I need you to keep it together and put a smile back on your face. If Sean isn't back in time, you're going to have to do the presentation by yourself. Will you be up to that?"

"I've got this, Martine. You take care of that woman," Caitlin insisted.

She and Paris had time for a glass of wine while they waited for Sean to return from speaking with the police. She was about to hunt him down when he re-entered the ballroom.

"See, he's fine," Paris said. "You take care of him,

I'll go find Martine. I don't like the looks of what is brewing with the SWAT Boyz in the corner."

"Thanks, Paris. For everything." Caitlin watched her date glad-hand his way through the crush of people, smiling at her the entire time. He didn't appear to be any worse for wear after his ordeal. He was almost to her when she spotted another incident in the making.

A gorgeous, petite redhead in a gold dress with a matching clutch, which probably cost as much as Caitlin's entire ensemble, was making a bee-line toward Sean with sheer predatory interest in her eyes. Caitlin recognized the black widow expression. She'd been at auditions with similar women. They reeked of attitude and trouble.

The look on Sean's face when he saw the redhead and the fact that he sped up to get to Caitlin before the other woman caught him made Caitlin want to snicker. Sean had no interest in talking to the new arrival and he made it as clear as he could without snubbing her outright. He dodged the kiss she tried to drop on his lips and she ended up performing an awkward air kiss.

"Megan, this is a surprise." It took him almost a minute to disentangle himself from her near kiss and handsy hug. To his credit, Caitlin had to admit it did appear like he was trying. He stepped back and wrapped his arms around Caitlin's waist. He couldn't be more taken if he'd stamped a "Property of" tattoo on his forehead.

"I've missed you, Sean. I haven't seen you since our weekend together in San Diego. I'm sorry I haven't called you back," Megan said.

How desperately bitchy to pull something like this in front of a man's date. Bitchy and dangerous, considering Caitlin was still coming down from the last incident. She coughed once to get their attention and plastered a smile on her face. "Sean, would you like to introduce us?"

She broke into a wide smile when he mouthed a desperate no at her before turning back to the redhead. "Caitlin, this is an old…may I introduce Megan. Megan Unger, this is Cait."

Caitlin could have gotten frostbite from the looks she got. She smiled bigger. "Hi, I'm Caitlin Kelly. Sorry to interrupt, but Sean and I have to get to work."

"Oh, Sean can wait a minute for a friend." Megan reached for his arm.

"No, he really can't." Caitlin tilted her head toward to podium at the front of the room where Martine was gesturing at them. "We're being paged." The waving turned frantic. "Urgently paged."

"Goodbye, Megan." Sean executed some kind of basketball fake and Caitlin found herself halfway across the room before she could blink. He didn't slow down as they darted around the other guests. "I am sorry about that. We used to…"

"I got that." She had the choice to laugh it off or get furious. Sean was obviously furious enough for the both of them. It would have been easy to judge the wicked blush he sported as embarrassment, but his frown and the furrow between his eyebrows spoke a different story. "I'm not mad at you. Megan was a bitch. I'm upset for you about that fan, but I'm not upset at you."

"Her? That was nothing. I'm still sorry about Megan, though. She's not usually so…"

Megan was definitely so. Caitlin would put money on it. Most men tended not to worry too much about personalities as long as the woman they were attached to put out.

They got to the small stage and Martine gave them a

quick once-over. "I wish you would have told me you were bringing a date, Sean. I would have made sure you were sitting together at the very least," she said. "I think we might be able to squeeze in a chair for her beside me and Paris."

"No, I'm not here with her. I'm with Caitlin. Megan didn't leave a lipstick mark, did she? It was her thing whenever we were in public." Sean scrubbed his cheek.

"A little TMI," Martine said as she inspected his face. "No, you're good. Are you two ready to do this?"

Caitlin nodded at Sean. "Yes, we're ready."

Chapter 5

SEAN stood behind the podium under protest. At the last minute he was forced into a deal he didn't like very much. He had to resort to bribery. If his little brain would shut up for five minutes, they could get through the guest speaker's introduction. If it did, his big brain promised to ask Caitlin what perfume she was wearing. Every time she pushed a lock of her hair behind her ear he caught of whiff of it. The scent was driving him to distraction.

He escorted Caitlin to their table and slid her chair in under her. While he had her where he wanted, he leaned forward and asked, "What's the name of your perfume?"

"Burberry. Why?"

"I like it. A lot." He would have played it cooler, but he thought he might be playing catch-up after Megan. "Are you okay?"

"Yeah, I think that went well. Although I am wondering why I got tapped for it." Her smile didn't waver when she said, "You, I can see. Chris, Nick, Layla, Glinda. Even Jason and Jessica. You guys have been there since the beginning. I haven't." She stared at him like she was waiting for an answer.

"I don't know why they chose us, but that's not what I was talking about. That scene with Megan. I'm really sorry."

"Don't worry about it. It's not like you pulled her into a broom closet and went at it."

"I have never done it in a broom closet. Ever." A photocopier room, and a gas station restroom. Never a broom closet. Sean looked into Caitlin's brown eyes, nearly black in the dim room, and realized those particular exploits seemed like they happened a million years ago.

He didn't have any problem remembering the first time he'd met her; she was sweaty and sand-covered after losing a beach volleyball game. Fuck, he was gone for her. He hadn't realized he had it so bad. It had been a pain in the ass to even get a first date with her. He liked that he'd had to work for it. It was a nice change from simply pointing into the crowd and crooking his finger. "Does this mean we're on track for a second date?" he asked. He hoped she said yes. He didn't have a back-up plan for now that didn't involve begging and pleading. Sean needed her to say yes.

"Don't you mean a first date?" she whispered back as the third benefactor of the night crossed the stage.

"How can you not count this as a first date? I provided dinner and entertainment." He scooted a little closer and wrapped his arm around the back of her chair. "I think tonight is going very well."

"My first-date bar is exceptionally high. If you want to count this one, we can, but we had better be done with bumps for the rest of the evening," Caitlin warned.

Sean refused to flinch at her glare. He'd worked too long and too hard to back off now.

"I definitely want to count this one. The rest of the night will go flawlessly. I promise."

"Okay, fine," she relented. "It's our first date."

"Does that mean I get a good-night kiss?"

"You have to push it, don't you?" Caitlin had that laughing tone back in her voice when she said it, and she also wore the same look of relief she got after a difficult scene ended well. But this wasn't the end; it was just the beginning. Sean had taken the long shot and made it. No risk, no reward. He felt like every winning cliché his coaches had ever spouted to him was true.

The ceremony portion of the evening finally ended and they had to make the rounds again. Sean wanted to get them out of there as quickly as possible. Not to take Caitlin home and end the evening with a kiss—that was the last thing on his to-do list. No, he wanted to get her alone for a minute without having to keep an eye on her and the two hundred people who were watching them.

He should have been watching the two hundred and first person.

At first he thought it was Caitlin. She had a sense of humor. When an arm reached out of the shadows and yanked him into the dark, empty room, Sean went with it. It would be just like her to cover his eyes and pull him into a dark corner to kiss him then walk away.

He'd spent hours, days, imagining what kissing Caitlin would be like. What her lips would feel like, how she would taste; the way she'd fit against him when he held her for real and not for camera angles. He knew it was going to be wonderful.

Wonderful was the wrong word. It was all…bad. She didn't fit right in his arms. Not from what he remembered when he'd had the chance to kiss her in front of the cameras. He'd give this kiss an eight out of ten for technical merit. Artistically he'd have to rate it a two: all form and no substance. A second thought crossed his mind and he started wondering when Caitlin had time to change her perfume.

Shit! Sean opened his eyes and saw a mass of perfectly highlighted red hair. He yanked his head back and looked down at Megan's beaming face. "Hi, lover."

Sean shoved her away and stepped back at the same

time. "What the fuck, Megan?"

"I couldn't get close enough to give you a proper hello earlier. Really, Sean, you let the studio saddle you with a date? I know it's been a few months, but you could have given me a call. We always have a good time." She moved forward and dropped her hand to his belt. "I know at least part of you remembers."

Whatever remnants of a hard-on Sean had from when he thought he was kissing Caitlin, vanished. "If I'd wanted to come here with you, I'd be here with you. Besides, aren't you seeing Don or Dale or one of the other SWAT Boyz at the moment?" Megan was a semi-professional groupie, which he had no trouble with. She was good at it and it had worked for both of them at the time. After she made her way through the available Olympus men, she moved on to the show that filmed in the soundstage next door. With her easy access to actors, Sean knew she held some kind of job with the studio. However, he couldn't remember what it was. If he ever knew. They hadn't talked much.

"We're fluid."

"Look, Megan, I'm interested in somebody else. I'm with Caitlin."

"You don't do 'interested.' You do fucking and not fucking." Her voice lost its playful, teasing tone.

"Now I do 'interested'." Each passing second had the hair on the back of Sean's neck rise a little more. It wasn't Megan's attitude; it hadn't changed. It was that his used to match. The thought of a nearly-nameless hook-up now did nothing for him anymore.

"With who? Caitlin Kelly? She's nobody. I have more useful connections than she does."

"I'm not with her for her connections."

She dropped her arms to her sides and stared into his

eyes. "You really are serious, aren't you?"

"I am."

"How about once more for the road, for old times' sake?" Before he could respond, she pressed a finger to his lips. "Not that. A good-bye kiss."

Sean did not hit women. Ever. Luckily he had no problem setting them aside hard and fast, and bolting for the door. He stepped into the hotel corridor and didn't spot anybody except a waiter by the kitchen door on his phone. Sean headed in the other direction. The last thing he needed was witnesses to his screw-up.

He needed to find Caitlin.

* * * *

She needed to find Sean.

It didn't count as her date ditching her if he'd been called away for another photo op. Caitlin had disappeared on Sean twice for the same reason, and the night was still young. Now she couldn't find him anywhere and time was getting short.

Martine had tracked her down in the ladies room, her usual cool exterior fractured by the news she had. "Two of the SWAT Boyz got into a fistfight in the lobby. Somebody called the cops before I could get there to deal with it. They were supposed to present the next check. I need an emergency replacement. Congratulations, you're it. You need to be ready to go on in five minutes."

"Are you crazy? Don't you want the guys to do it? People at least know them," Caitlin protested.

"No. Jay Wilson spoke to Robert Clancy who called me. He wants to do it with you."

"Jay Wilson of Mastersounds? No, obviously not. A regular guy named Jay Wilson who works for a charity and is a fan of the show. Right. We can do that. I have to find Sean," Caitlin said, already planning what she needed to do and say in her head. She'd had a split-second panic attack when Martine mentioned Jay Wilson before she realized the real Jay Wilson would have no idea who she was.

"You aren't presenting with Sean."

"I'm not? Who am I presenting with?" Caitlin should find Paris. Martine needed to calm down because she wasn't making any sense at all.

"Jay Wilson of Mastersounds."

Mastersounds's first single from their third album had cracked the top ten and Jay Wilson was the reason the video was still climbing the charts. The lead singer was built like a sexy tank and had the lung capacity to match. He was a powerhouse singer and Caitlin was a huge fan. "Are you sure he meant me? I've never met the man."

"He says he likes your music. Which we will be discussing later. In detail. First you need to do this presentation. Are you ready for this?"

Master-freaking-sounds. The guys in the band were going to be so jealous. "Absolutely."

"Great. Let's go."

"Can you find Sean for me and tell him what's happening?" Caitlin tried to smooth the creases out of her skirt; sitting for two hours left unavoidable wrinkles. She gave it a hopeful tug, but it did nothing. She was going to meet Jay Wilson looking like she slept in her car. Caitlin shook off the negativity and tried again. She was going to meet Jay Wilson. That was better.

"Good skirt length, by the way," Martine complimented. "Skin, but not too much. It suits you and Psyche."

"It's not too long? I don't want to be goodie-goodie. Sex sells," Caitlin said.

"Sexy sells," Martine corrected. "You look great. Now let's go."

Martine kept an iron grip on her arm as she half-dragged her through the lobby. Caitlin trailed along willingly until she hit the brakes when Sean turned the corner. "Where have you been?" she asked as she straightened his tie.

"I was tied up. What's going on?"

Martine tugged until they started moving again. "I need Caitlin to do another presentation with Jay Wilson. Like, now."

Desperate to keep some dignity, Caitlin stopped fighting and squared her shoulders as they headed back to the ballroom.

"The lead singer of Mastersounds?" Sean asked, an echo of her response. "That is too cool. You have to introduce me."

She was surprised, although she didn't know why. She had no idea what kind of music Sean liked. It was entirely possible he was a rock fan. It always took her by surprise when she remembered famous people were people. They had their own idols and got star-struck as much as anyone else. "Sure, we'll be best buds by the time we're done," she said.

Then the singer was there. "Hi, I'm Jay Wilson."

"Caitlin Kelly. Nice to meet you."

"Okay, they're ready for you," Martine announced as she peeked through the door.

Her co-presenter offered Caitlin his arm. She barely had time to see Sean shoot her a thumbs-up before she was led inside. Caitlin smiled and flirted and posed for the photographers with the man of the moment.

Sean reappeared as they left the podium. He wrapped his arm around Caitlin's waist. If he were any more possessive, he'd be pissing on my leg to mark me. "Great job, you two. I didn't realize you were friends."

"Friend, no. Fan, yes," Jay said. "I know you are both doing the network thing tonight, so I won't keep Caitlin any longer than I have to. Maybe I can catch a Charlie Oscar Echo show someday while I'm in town."

Her mouth was moving before her brain engaged. "We're playing this weekend," she said. The guys would die if she got Mastersounds to one of their shows.

"I'm flying out tomorrow. Maybe next time."

"Likewise," she said. Now that she was gainfully employed, she could afford luxuries like concert tickets. Jay's show would be worth any price. If Sean were a fan, she'd take him too.

When it was back to Sean and her, she knew she owed him an apology. "I'm sorry. I didn't mean to ask him to a concert in front of you. He said he liked my music and I panicked!" She couldn't believe she'd been so incredibly rude.

Sean pulled her into a hug, dropping his forehead to hers. "How about we never mention what happened tonight again. Megan and Jay who?"

"Deal." Sean scored huge brownie points for his understanding. He wasn't responsible for Megan's behavior, but Caitlin was responsible for hers. The night was twistier than a rollercoaster. She was lucky Sean was along to hold onto during the ride.

"Okay, back to work."

Caitlin shook more hands and smiled for more pictures. Sean was never more than a few steps away. For a working date, he certainly showed a girl a good time.

Chapter 6

SEAN hadn't been this nervous since he'd taken Julie Landes to junior prom, while knowing he was going to get lucky afterward. It was their first official non-working date, everything was going to be flawless. It had to be.

He pulled up behind the Duncan Building and studied the second floor windows. Caitlin's apartment was in a decent area, although a place above a dance studio wasn't what he expected for an actress on the rise. He lifted the delicate red and white flowers off the passenger seat and carried them carefully. Caitlin buzzed him right up; telling him her door was open.

Her neighbor, a solid-looking guy with long hair, watched him through a crack in his door until Caitlin called out a greeting and Sean let himself into her apartment. "Did you know you've got a stalker?" he asked once he ensured the deadbolt was in place.

"I've got a what?" That wasn't an I-didn't-hear-you question. She was giving him a chance to change what he said. Sean knew that tone.

"The scary-looking guy across the hall. He was watching your place and your door was open," he elaborated.

"He's not a stalker. That's Marcus," Caitlin said. Apparently having a neighbor spying on her was nothing to be concerned about because she quickly moved on. Caitlin pointed at the sleek bouquet in his arms and gasped. "Are those gorgeous things for me?"

She got him flustered faster than anyone he'd ever met. He handed the flowers over and checked out her small apartment. "Did you just move in?" he asked when he spotted a wall of boxes in her living room.

"A few months ago," she replied from the kitchen. "Isn't this place great? It's twice the size of my last apartment, which was a bachelor suite. I jumped on this unit as soon as Ashleigh told me about it."

Now it made sense. This was her friend's building. Sean knew they were insanely tight with each other. Of course she would support her friend, and Ashleigh would want to rent to a person she knew she could trust.

Caitlin came out holding a tall, narrow vase. She'd done the thing with the flowers where they looked like a real display instead of being fluffed after taking them out of their wrapper.

"You made those look nice," he told her. "Although not as nice as you." The flowers were pretty; she was stunning. He liked that Caitlin was a dress girl. He appreciated femininity. She also had the legs to make really short hemlines work for her. "Are you ready to go?"

"Where are we off to?" she asked.

"Lowell's Bar." It was upper end, but not outrageously formal. His shirt and tie were enough to get him through the door, and nobody would be dumb enough to deny Caitlin entrance. It also had some of the best steaks in town. Shit. "You aren't vegetarian, are you?" he asked when they got to his car.

"Only when I have to be."

Thank God for that. He wasn't willing to give up steak for anybody.

Sean loved to drive after the sun went down. The artificial glow kept the darkness in the city at bay. It made up for not being able to see real stars. The open night sky was what he missed most about Wyoming. When he mentioned it to Caitlin, she laughed.

"I'm not laughing at you. I'm the complete opposite. I love the city. I spent far too much of my time restricted to military bases because of safety concerns. I need the noise and the crowds."

He eyed the oncoming vehicles and calculated the break he'd need to cross the street and pull up to the restaurant's valet entrance. "You picked a good career then." He saw his chance and gripped the wheel. Then he spotted something on the sidewalk that had him slamming on the brakes.

"What's wrong?" Caitlin asked.

"I...We need to drive around the block." He ignored the look on her face as he eased back into the flow of traffic. He wanted to do another drive-by to make sure he saw what he thought he saw. He was probably being paranoid. There was no reason to assume the over-exuberant fan who jumped him at the banquet would be at the entrance of the restaurant waiting for him. She could be waiting for her date. It likely wasn't her at all.

"Sean?"

"It's nothing."

"Did you not hear me say I spent my childhood living with safety concerns? What did you see?"

"I think I saw the woman from the banquet last week."

"Megan?"

"No, the other one. In the ballroom. Who kissed me."

He had to duck Caitlin's elbow as she twisted in her seat. "That bitch was there? Where's my phone?"

"Why do you need your phone?"

"To call the cops because she's violating her

restraining order?"

Sean sighed. "I didn't get an R.O., Caitlin. She just got a little overwhelmed. It happens." It wasn't a big deal. He wouldn't have hesitated if he'd had anybody other than Caitlin in the car with him. Fans were part of the deal.

"She's stalking you."

Caitlin sounded seriously pissed. He wasn't sure if it was at him or at the hapless woman who he prayed was gone by the time they swung back around to the restaurant. He didn't want to be responsible for Caitlin going psycho on her ass. "I'm fine. She apologized and said it wouldn't happen again."

"Shit, Sean. You need to be more careful."

That sounded more protective than anything else. "It'll be fine, Caitlin." He made the final turn and studied the street. "She's not there anymore. I must have been seeing things."

Supper was good, not great. Caitlin seemed guarded the entire time. Not against him—in general. If he looked past the tension, things went better than he'd hoped. They were as compatible as he'd thought they'd be. Caitlin didn't start to relax until they moved to the Agave Lounge off the beach for a drink. Sean slid his stool closer to her and draped his arm on her backrest. "You doing okay?"

She did a stretchy, not quite yawn thing, which meant she rubbed one of her shoulders against his chest. She might as well have used a flamethrower for the response she got. His skin burned painfully hot where she'd touched him. It took a second to focus on her verbal answer. "Yeah. I didn't realize you didn't take stuff like that as seriously as I did. It's not an issue now. You're a pretty good date, Sean."

"Thank you. Does that mean you want to do it again?" Yes, he was pushing. He'd have to apologize to Chris for laughing when Chris had said after only one day with Sydney that he'd known they'd work. Sean felt the exact same way, with the benefit of already knowing what holding and kissing Caitlin would be like. Despite the clinical detachment of doing it over and over again in front of an audience, he knew how his body reacted to hers. Her shiver from him tracing the skin on the back of her neck was a good sign it was reciprocated. "Tomorrow?" They weren't working the next day.

Caitlin shook her head. "I'm working tomorrow. Charlie has a gig at the Diamond Room." The silence stretched between them until she added, "Unless you'd like to come see us play? I'd be able to see you between sets, though. It might be boring for you. You could bring some friends."

Sean had done his research. He'd downloaded the band's album and played it in his car. It hadn't grabbed him. However, it was probably worth another listen if Jay Wilson liked it. Caitlin didn't talk about the band much when she was at work. He'd assumed it was just another way for her to make some money before she started working full-time as an actress. He'd apparently underestimated the importance the band held in her life. "Sure. If you leave some tickets at the door, I'll be there."

* * * *

Caitlin peeked out of the wings into the crowd on the Diamond Room dance floor and got caught for the fourth time. "Cait, what do you think you're doing?" Peter asked her. "Who are you looking for?"

"Nobody." What had she been thinking? Bringing a date to a show? And with three honorary big brothers in the building? If they found him lacking, Sean wouldn't stand a chance.

Not that they should find anything lacking. She didn't. The boy was hot; the whole package. He got her lady parts tingling—something Caitlin wouldn't share with the band. And when he was with her, he was fully with her. He seared her with his focus and it was undeniable she had his complete attention. It was sexy as hell.

Sean wasn't in the audience. He hadn't picked up the tickets she'd left at the door and the band was about to go on. She had no idea why he'd changed his mind.

"Cait-girl, is your head in the game?" Bobby asked as he handed over her guitar.

"Yeah, I'm good." She didn't know what Sean's play was and she didn't have the time to figure it out. She closed her eyes and pulled Caitlin the Rocker to the foreground. "We're starting with Break, right?"

"Same set as our last show," Bobby said.

"Got it. Let's go have some fun."

Caitlin loved being on stage. Loved it. Singing, dancing, acting, she didn't care which. As long as she could perform—preferably in front of an audience—she was in heaven. No matter how tired or upset she was. Once the spotlight hit her she was on. The rest of the world faded away.

The audience tonight was huge. It was by far the biggest turn-out they'd ever had. Caitlin let the frenetic energy in the club pour over her as she grabbed her guitar. Then she played.

She and Greg were on fire as he led the band through the first set. The room had an artificial calm when they played Watching Him Watching Her. Caitlin didn't understand it because the guys hadn't said anything about releasing the video. Though, to be fair, these days she was so busy she might not know even if they'd sent her an email. She made a mental note to check her inbox again and fell back into the music.

That feeling was why she didn't notice Sean in the crowd until they were headed off-stage forty minutes later. A whistle pierced the loud club noise. She turned to find its source and saw him waving from behind a velvet rope in the VIP section to the side of the stage.

He showed! Caitlin had almost convinced herself that she didn't care, but by the way her heart was pounding, she wasn't fooling herself in the slightest. She held up her hand to tell him she needed five minutes. She could leave the guys to their bucket of beer in the dressing room, visit with Sean, and come back just before they had to do their second set. If she timed it right, it wouldn't give them any time to grill her about her date. If Sean did the neck rub thing again while they were talking, she'd have to change her underwear before she got back on stage. The touch of that man's hands undid her.

Her grand plan would have worked too if he hadn't left an invitation for the entire band to join him.

Now she was stuck in a corner, by herself, guzzling a Perrier, while her guys were grilling her boyfriend on his basketball knowledge for their March Madness drafts. He'd barely said hi to her before her band mates mobbed the former point guard. There was no kiss hello, no whispering in her ear. And definitely no neck rub. Assholes. All of them.

She'd forgotten Sean wasn't half bad as an actor. As the guys filed back toward the stage, Sean caught her arm before she cleared the rope. "Why didn't you save me from that? I came here to see you," he growled in her ear.

"You're the one who invited them," Caitlin said.

"I wanted to meet them for a minute. I didn't know they wanted to stick around and talk b-ball. I didn't get to spend any time with you at all."

That admission made up for a good part of his lack of intention. She knew how annoying the guys could be, even when they didn't mean to. "Are you going to hang around after our second set?"

"Are you going to let me take you home?" Sean asked.

"I have my own car. I'll invite you in for a drink if you want to meet me at my place," she offered. She never fell asleep right after a show. The company would be nice while she came down from her performance high.

"Then, yes."

The next hour flew by. Caitlin had never been more efficient in breaking down gear and loading the band's various vehicles. "Bobby, get in the car. I want to go home." The sooner she dropped him off and said good night, the sooner she could say hello to Sean.

The blond drummer shook his head. "I'll get my own ride. It's date night."

"You have a date?"

"No, but you do."

Peter set down his amp. "Wait. Who's Caitlin seeing?"

"You'll pay for this, Bobby-o. Next time," she threatened. At the moment, she had a clear shot at a getaway. She went for it. Her tires squealed a little as she tore out of the parking lot.

Chapter 7

SO that was a Charlie Oscar Echo show.

Sean liked it. He'd been way off on the quality an indie band could put out. They were good enough to deserve the interest they were getting. Their online presence had exploded since the last time he'd looked. After "Break" was released, their schedule for upcoming performances had filled in considerably. He'd listened to their album again while he waited in the dark for Caitlin to finish loading her car. It wasn't stalking. He could wait for her at her apartment, looking suspicious while he staked out a single woman's apartment after midnight, or he could protectively follow her home from her job late at night and join her upstairs like he'd been invited to do.

Except he wasn't the only one waiting for her. There was another car in the lot and another person sitting with their interior light off. Sean couldn't make out the figure. He also couldn't read the dirty license plate. It could be a bar employee or someone waiting to pick up a friend, but he didn't think so. Unlike with him, there was no give-away glow from an active cell phone, and no music playing through an open window. They just sat there, waiting.

He was pleased to see Caitlin didn't walk to her vehicle alone. The band talked for a bit before she jumped into her truck. His phone pinged and he saw she'd sent him a text. Be home in 30.

He smiled as he texted back Right behind you. He flashed his headlights when he saw her scan the parking lot. She tapped her horn when she drove past him and he followed her. The mystery car must have been waiting for somebody else since it didn't move.

Marcus peeked out his apartment door again when he heard them in the hall. Sean wanted to say something. Caitlin didn't give him a chance. She gave the guy a wave and an "I'm good," and he shut the door. So, not a stalker. He still had his eye on Caitlin. Sean didn't approve.

"Jack Daniels?" Caitlin asked.

Sean had come out of the bathroom to find Caitlin changed out of the black leather pants and black tank top she'd worn on stage into a pair of low-cut jeans and a tight pink sweater. His brain was too busy to hear the question as he tried to figure out how covering more skin made her sexier. "What?"

"Are you a Jack man?" Caitlin repeated.

"Yes, thanks."

Caitlin handed him a glass and kept a bottle of beer for herself. "What did you think of the show?"

"Loved it. Loved you. I had no idea you could play like that." Despite the talk about equality, women in bands were a rarity. Women on bass guitar were slightly more common than unicorns. "Tell me about Not Quite Home. It sounds like a very personal song." Personal was an understatement. It was an outright baby-come-back ballad which Gregory Mills sang directly to Caitlin. After the first verse, Sean was ready to storm the stage to tell the lead singer he'd missed his shot and Caitlin had moved on. The whole touchy-feely back and forth on stage was way too practiced and intimate for his comfort level.

"Good ear. Greg wrote it as an engagement present when he was in Afghanistan."

"You two were engaged?" That news flipped a switch in his head. He hated the fact the singer had had his hands on Caitlin as part of their act. Knowing there was something behind the familiarity was out of line when she was dating somebody else. Kind of like getting caught kissing an ex, although in his case he did it by accident and he didn't rub her face in it.

Caitlin sprayed her drink down her top. "To each other? No. Fuck, no. That would be like incest or something. Greg was engaged to a nurse while he was overseas before she dumped him. Now I need to change again. I'll be right back."

The split second he had to relax after her vicious denial of a relationship with the other man died a fast death when she finished her thought. "I was engaged to a jump school instructor who offered me a white picket fence and a dog," she called from the bedroom.

What the fuck? Sean never once pictured Caitlin as the suburban family type. "What happened?"

She returned in an even tighter peach shirt. "Do I look like I want a dog and a white picket fence? Neil was a good guy. Unfortunately we weren't headed in the same direction long term. Last I heard, he found a pretty little nurse and was living the dream."

"Greg's nurse?" It would explain a couple of the other songs on the album. He hoped Caitlin didn't have a hand in writing them. Angry and bitter didn't begin to touch it. The kind of pain the band sang about took a long time to work through, and he'd waited long enough for his shot with her.

"No. I don't know her. I sent a congratulations card at the time. It was a few years ago. I never understood how people could stay friends after a break-up. When it's over, it should be over."

That was all the ex-boyfriend talk Sean could handle for one evening. He wanted Caitlin to think about him. "So what's your usual routine after a show?"

She hesitated, looking at the chair across the coffee table from him, and made her decision. She dropped down beside him on the sofa. "Usually, I come home by myself and I'm wired up. I have to do something to relax or I can't sleep."

Sean shifted his hand from the back cushion to Caitlin's neck and her head fell forward an inch.

"I should tell you to stop. It feels too good," she murmured.

That was a spot to remember then. "Why would you want to stop something that feels good?" His thumb caught a lock of her hair and he pulled on it gently until she lifted her face. The heat in her eyes made him skip his next comment and go for it.

Fuck. She lit up like a firework when he touched her. He'd waited too long to play games. Sean fisted her hair and kept Caitlin exactly where he wanted while he finally kissed her for real. Her mouth was an instant addiction, soft and sweet and welcoming. He probed with his tongue and she responded by curling her nails into his biceps.

He was inside her mouth and she was under his skin, and she was still too far away. He let go of her hair long enough to grab her hips and slide her across his legs until she straddled him. His straining cock was tight against the heat of her V. The pressure of her falling into him almost had him coming in his pants. Sean pulled her closer and bit her lip to share the pleasurable pain.

"No," he ordered when she leaned away. Then he saw her hands hooked under the hem of her shirt. "Okay, go ahead."

She'd barely revealed the lace at the bottom of her

bra when screaming erupted from the hall. "Get the fuck out of here!" was repeated and an air horn split the air. "You think I won't pull the trigger? Move it, you fucker!"

Caitlin scrambled off his lap. "That's Marcus." Before he could stop her, she ran to the shelf beside the door and grabbed a small, metal tube.

"What do you think you're doing?" he demanded.

"Protecting myself. Do you want to move?"

"You aren't going out there." The psycho across the hall was threatening to shoot people. Sean didn't care how well Caitlin could take care of herself. He wasn't going to step aside and let her run into harm's way.

"What's going on?" she hollered through the door since he wouldn't let her pass.

"Babe, you better get your honey out here. Somebody tried to break into his ride."

Sean's hand hit the doorknob a second before hers. He wasn't about to let her go first. Caitlin's nosy neighbor waited for them in the hall. "I was looking out the window and saw somebody crouched by your car. They took off when I hit them with my spotlight." The shorter man waved a piece of equipment at them. "I don't know how long they were there or if they got in. Do you want me to call the cops?"

Caitlin held her out free hand. "Gimme the flashlight, Marky-Mark."

It was then that Sean realized her neighbor was armed. "Cait, maybe you should wait in your apartment."

"I'm fine, Sean. Marky-Mark said they were gone. He can watch from the window while we check out the damage."

"Do you trust this guy? Who is he?" he asked.

"I'm Marcus Bolling. Babe, your guys aren't usually

this slow."

"Give us a break. We were distracted." She snatched the flashlight and bolted for the stairs. "If my car is damaged, there's going to be yelling."

Sean did the yelling. Caitlin's pick-up was untouched. His midnight-blue Maserati was beat to shit. Sean supposed he should be grateful it was only the driver's door, but he wasn't. It looked like somebody had keyed the panel to hell before they kicked it in. Fuckingpieceofshitpunkassfucker. Caitlin held the light for him while he took pictures with his phone.

"I'm sorry about your car, Sean."

His grumbling wasn't all about the car. "Why are you flirting with him?"

"Who? What flirting?"

"He calls you babe. You called him Marky-Mark. What's that about?"

"That's not flirting. Marcus calls me babe because he knows it pisses me off. I call him Marky-Mark because Russ said it would piss him off. I don't care how good he is at fixing my Wi-Fi, Marcus can be a real dick."

"Russ Vukovich knows him?"

"Yeah, they work together." She crouched down to get a better look at his car. "Do you have a good body shop? Because I know a guy."

Of course she knows a guy. She was apparently on a first name basis with every male in the greater Los Angeles area. Caitlin spending time with her girls was great, especially since he knew most of them and they were dating his buddies. Her naivety regarding most of the guys she called friends would be cute if she weren't under the mistaken impression they didn't want to fuck her. He was the one who was going to be fending them off once they found out she was off the market.

"It's okay. I know a guy too." He didn't want to meet one more asshole who would probably hug her when she walked through the door.

"This was a great mood-killer. Do you think we are ever going to have an uneventful date?"

Sean knew what she meant, but he couldn't agree. He hooked her belt with his finger. He had every intention of kissing her—at least until he spotted Marcus peering down from his apartment window. Before he pulled away, he flipped the guy the bird behind Caitlin's back. "I hope our next date is going to be eventful." He tugged her against his bulging crotch. "Very, very eventful."

* * * *

Caitlin was grateful the invading forces waited until noon. They also brought coffee and Caitlin's weekly cheat breakfast so she didn't growl too much when she buzzed them in and retreated back to her nest on the sofa.

Sydney Richardson took ownership of Caitlin's old beanbag chair, dragging it over to the coffee table. Sydney was always diligent about not scattering cranberry scone crumbs while she ate. She tossed the other Bella Bean bag to Caitlin. "I am not keeping that disgusting thing any longer than necessary. It's a crime against baked goods."

"It's a cheese scone. Yummy cheddar," Caitlin choked out over a mouthful of deliciousness.

"Cheese and baking should never be combined. Never," Sydney insisted. She held up a finger. "Unless it's cream cheese in a Danish or cheesecake. Not hard cheeses and innocent scones."

Ashleigh Jessup never bothered with breakfast accessories. She had all the calories she needed in her coffee. Caitlin was sure the extra-large cup was at least half whipped cream and caramel sauce. Then again, Ashleigh was a dance instructor and burned more calories in one day than most office workers did in a week. "You have a problem when it comes to pastries, Syd."

"I do not. I love them. It's not a problem."

Caitlin was halfway through her French roast when she realized the other women in the room were watching her silently. "What?"

"We're waiting for our after-action report," Sydney said.

"After-nookie report," Ashleigh corrected.

"What nookie?" Caitlin asked.

"Oh, no. Is Sean all talk and no action? Is that why he's never seen with the same girl twice?" Sydney was distraught enough to set down her scone. Caitlin loved her friends. She'd love them more if they stayed out of her sex life.

"No, if that were the case, one of them would have said something," Ashleigh said. "Maybe it was a one-time problem. Caitlin did tell us it had been a really long week."

"For fuck's sake, Sean doesn't have a problem. I was cock-blocked by my neighbor, okay?"

"I wasn't even home!" Ashleigh protested. "I was at Nick's last night."

"Not you. Marcus. Sean and I were getting comfortable and Marcus hit an air horn and called us into the hallway because he thought he saw somebody breaking into Sean's car." Caitlin sighed. Sean left after they documented the damage to his vehicle, the mood having been thoroughly broken. However, Caitlin had been much too wired to go to sleep immediately. Add in Sean getting her wound up with no follow-through and she'd had a very rough time relaxing enough to doze off, even with the use of her battery-operated sleep aid in her nightstand drawer.

"You can't catch a break with Sean, can you?" Ashleigh fought back a laugh. "It's not easy dating an actor. I think they have weird shit magnets surgically implanted when they get their SAG cards." She would know. Ashleigh had begun dating Nick Thurston the previous summer while the Olympus actor was on hiatus between seasons. She'd immediately been sucked into a nasty battle with her old boss—who was also Nick's previous girlfriend—which almost resulted in her losing both her studio and Nick. It took months and moving to a new building to sort everything out. Thankfully, their relationship was calmer now.

"You do know I'm an actress," Caitlin protested.

"Thus proving her point," Sydney said. "Seriously, though, are you all right? Is Sean? What happened to his car?"

"Somebody keyed the driver's side. They didn't touch my piece of shit. Or Marcus'."

"Well, you two don't drive Maseratis. If I wanted to ruin somebody's day, I'd target Richie Rich first too," Sydney continued.

"Why didn't you call me? I'm your landlord," Ashleigh said, her latte abandoned.

"It was one in the morning and you were at Nick's. The person ran away and nobody got a good look beyond "someone in a hoodie." Sean's going to file a report today and I said I'd tell you when you came over. Now I'm telling you."

"My insurance rates are going to go through the roof," Ashleigh moaned.

"I think Marcus is going to hunt you down later and discuss motion sensor lights for behind the building and the side entrance," Caitlin warned her. When she'd moved into the building, Ashleigh had claimed the second-floor, two-bedroom suite for herself by reason of owning the building and getting first pick. Caitlin got to choose between the two remaining single bedroom apartments. The other suite had stayed unrented for two months until Ashleigh found another tenant both she and Caitlin were comfortable with. Marcus was a non-smoker, had a sterling credit rating, and, most importantly, was a trusted friend of a friend. Learning he worked as a consultant for Pacific Personal Security sealed the deal. Who wouldn't want an armed bodyguard living in their building?

"Maybe I can offer him a reduction on his rent if he does it," Ashleigh said.

"I'm all for more security and you being safe, but can we please get back to the sex?" Sydney asked. "Because somebody should be having some."

This was news. "Why? Is Chris having performance issues?" Caitlin asked. Payback was sweet.

"No! And I won't ask about Sean again if you promise not to ask about Chris. He's been as sick as a dog. I left him sleeping this morning. Remind me to call in an hour to check on him," Sydney said. Caitlin almost felt bad about giving her a hard time; Sydney was the reason Caitlin had met Chris Peck and Robert Clancy and was now gainfully employed. Syd and Chris had been together for a year now and showed no sign of slowing down.

"At least we're in the same boat," Caitlin commiserated.

"Speak for yourselves," Ashleigh said. "Some of us are doing fine, thank you very much."

Caitlin laughed. If anything was going to make her

feel better about not going all the way with Sean, it was going to be these two. "I think I'm glad Marcus interrupted us. We were rushing things a bit." It gave her a chance to take a breath. She knew Sean was hot; she'd know that for months. Getting up close and personal had fried her synapses. The fact Sean had claimed not to be the man-whore he used to be didn't mean she should dive into something without testing the waters.

Despite what the girls thought, she wasn't gun-shy about getting serious. Caitlin wanted a relationship, provided both sides knew what they were getting into. Neil had wanted a nice family woman, while Caitlin wanted someone who was as career-minded as she was so they could support each other on their way to the top. Neither of them changed their minds like the other had hoped, so they had had to make a decision. For Caitlin, it was moving on.

Sean hadn't breathed a word about wanting a family in the not-too-distant future. Or stepping out of the spotlight and settling down. He was a perfect match, as long as he held the line. Caitlin wanted to give him time to see if that changed before she considered anything long-term. Once she was certain of that, she'd happily take herself off the leash.

"I don't think you're rushing," Sydney said. "We need to get you laid. Where's Sean now?"

"Are you even listening to me?"

Chapter 8

SEAN had never done this before. It could go either way. Although, the more he thought about it, his odds were leaning heavily in favor of one outcome: utter disaster. He didn't know if Caitlin liked basketball, let alone if she would be interested in sitting through an entire game with a volatile crowd whose team had already lost its shot at the playoffs.

He wished he would have thought of it before he arrived at her place with the tickets in his back pocket. The last time he was here, they'd almost made it to her bedroom for a very happy ending to their first-date do-over. He'd told her to expect a surprise. If she answered the door in lingerie and he had to explain why he had to turn her down, he was going to be beyond pissed at himself.

Somebody must have tipped her off, because Caitlin answered the door in jeans and a—"Are you wearing an alumni sweatshirt?"

She looked down at her chest and nodded. "Apparently."

"Did one of the guys tell you where we were going?" Sean asked.

"They didn't have to. You aren't exactly Mr. Subtle. You sent out an email inviting the cast and crew to join your March Madness pool and today is the last regular season game. I also heard you turn down three offers to buy your tickets. I thought us going to the basketball game was a good bet."

"The pool is for charity," Sean protested. Well, half went to charity, specifically Layla Andrews's Lights! Camera! Action! Drama Camp. The other half went to the winner. Back to the matter at hand. "How much of a basketball fan are you?"

She lifted her sweater and flashed her chest. Unfortunately it was covered with a T-shirt sporting a bear giving everyone a thumbs-up. "I was more of a volleyball fan. I would hit a game or two when I had tickets. Of course, I was in no-man's land. I assume yours are a little closer to the action."

Sean wanted to brag, but he had a feeling it wouldn't go over well. The tickets in his pocket were for just off court-side. "They aren't bad."

* * * *

At half-time, Sean was second-guessing his date idea again. Caitlin seemed to be having a good time…when he remembered to check. He kept getting caught up in the action on the court. The game was intense even if the standings wouldn't change for either team: one of them was long out of the running, and the other was practically guaranteed a place in the quarter-finals. The players were good. The coaching was phenomenal. Sean had the uncomfortable suspicion he'd missed a couple hand-on-his-thigh moments when he was too involved with the game. In the meantime, he had to make up for his lack of attention.

"Would you like anything to eat?" he asked as the stands cleared.

"No thanks. I'd love a drink though."

Sean kept his hand on the small of her back as they maneuvered through the crowd, hooking his finger through her belt loop to keep them from getting separated. He liked having her within reach. He liked that she liked being within reach even more. Despite the crush, they'd spent two whole hours together without any more interruptions than could be expected at a sporting event.

"Whoa, are you Sean Glenn?" an itty-bitty freshman-looking girl asked him.

"It's him. This is so cool! Can we get a picture with you?" her friend asked.

Caitlin slipped out of his grasp, nodding to give him permission to ignore her in favor of his fans. He kept an eye on her when she staked out a piece of wall to wait him out. This was the first time he felt the slightest resentment toward his fame. He didn't want to have to give Caitlin up, even for a minute. It was hard enough to find time with her during the week; filming days were too long on their own. Anything beyond a quick meal at the end of the day meant they both paid the next morning on set. He'd waited a week to take her to this game. He'd already fucked up by ignoring her during the first half. If he didn't get it together, the next hour would end with a kiss goodbye in the parking lot. He was not going to suffer one more night of blue balls.

The clock ticking down to the start of the third quarter worked in his favor. He dealt with two more sets of pictures, shuffling closer to the arena entrance each time, before the crowd moved on. It was great Caitlin understood his need to set her aside for a moment to work the crowd. It was both a perk and a problem with fame.

"Sorry about that," he apologized on the way back to their seats.

"Don't worry. You didn't have a chance to eat, though," she whispered into his ear.

Sean inhaled as he wrapped his arm around her shoulders and pulled her close enough to do the same. He caught the faintest scent of lemon. "So, does that mean I can take you out for dinner afterward?"

He bit back a groan when she put her hand on his thigh and squeezed. "Works for me."

Four thigh squeezes—five if he counted the one during the half-court shot that hung in the air for-fucking-ever before dropping through the net, but Sean figured that was an actual game-induced touch; three cuddles into his chest to get settled after she jumped to her feet to cheer for various scoring chances; and one moan that vibrated through her ribcage when he rubbed the same spot on her neck which had set her off the weekend before. He couldn't risk a second touch on her soft, bare skin. Not if he wanted to be able to walk back to the car after the game. He was going to remember that spot until the day he died.

After the final buzzer sounded, Sean asked a question he didn't want the answer to. "Where would you like to go for dinner?" Anywhere she chose was going to take too long, and no restaurant worth taking Caitlin to would let him move her hand up his thigh to where he really wanted to be rubbed and squeezed.

"My place. We can order in."

Fuck, Caitlin was perfect.

* * * *

She'd done it. She'd made it through an entire basketball game without snarky commentary or slipping into a coma. It was a dirty trick, but she'd hoped she'd be able to tease Sean enough to convince him to leave at halftime. She failed miserably. He seemed completely immune to her charms. She'd underestimated how serious he was about his college ball. The dude was fanatical.

Something changed during the second half and Caitlin had tried to figure out what it was. When she had grabbed Sean's knee during the thirty seconds she'd actually been paying attention to the play in front of her, he caught her hand and held it. She'd definitely got his attention when she squeezed his leg a few moments later. He reciprocated and, damn, that boy's hands were lethal weapons when it came to her panties. It didn't matter if his eyes were looking in the other direction.

"Sean, I have to tell you, rush hour has never been so much fun." She squealed as he unhooked her bra through her T-shirt. It was only fair. He'd almost missed the on-ramp when she'd pulled his belt out of the loops on his jeans. When she said she'd "save it for later," Sean threatened to make her pay for any speeding tickets he got while racing back to her place.

"We have got to start carpooling," he said.

"Do you want me to tell you what I'm thinking should go down at my place?" Caitlin asked.

"Besides you?"

"Don't worry, I'm not greedy. I'm going to make sure you have a turn," she said, before she winced at the screeching tires as Sean hit the brakes again. "On second thought, you concentrate on driving and I'll sit here quietly and think about the bad, bad things I'm going to do to you."

"I'd say I hate you, but frankly, I'm way too turned on to be mad," Sean growled.

Caitlin shrugged off her bra, pulled it out of her shirt sleeve, and set the lacy, navy scraps in her lap. She didn't look at him as she slowly folded it and slid it into her hoodie pocket.

"I take it back," Sean said. "I hate you."

He obviously forgave her quickly enough once they were inside her apartment. "I'm five seconds from stripping you down and taking you on the sofa. Speak now or hold your peace 'til I'm done with you," he warned her.

"My bed has better springs than the sofa," was all she had time to say before he was on her.

Caitlin lost track of time during their race from the front door to the bedroom. At some point her jeans came off and Sean put both of his huge hands on her ass and lifted her so she could wrap her legs around his waist. His protruding jeans chafed through her thin lace panties. When she pushed him away, Sean grunted and pulled her tighter against him. "No backing off now," he said before he dropped her on the bed, pinning her against the mattress.

"Your zipper," she muttered.

"You think I can't feel it. It's leaving teeth marks on my dick. If I've got teeth at my dick they should be yours doing exactly what I tell you to."

"Do you want to talk, or do you want to get naked?"

Goddamn, he tasted good. He smelled even better when he buried his face in her neck. Caitlin threaded her fingers into his thick hair while he kicked himself free of his jeans. He collapsed against her and lay there for a moment, skin to skin, breathing hard. "Shit. My condoms are in my wallet in my pocket."

"You get those. I'll get out of these," Caitlin offered. She slid her hand under her waistband.

Sean grabbed her hand and held it still. "No, I'm going to take those off. Don't move."

She stared at him, defiantly tracing the edge of the lace, one finger on top of the material and the other underneath, sliding them slowly over her hips.

"Cait," he warned her, "I'm not playing around with you tonight."

"But I like to play."

She was never this playful during sex. Happy and energetic, sure, but Sean's bossy orders stirred up some sass and she liked how he dealt with it. He was by far the physically biggest man she'd ever had in her bed. The shock that speared down her spine when he pinned her to the mattress promised to be an excellent sign of what she hoped would come.

Sean paused at the foot of the bed. He stared down at Caitlin, who was sprawled across the pink sheets of her unmade bed. "Goddamn, you are gorgeous." Instead of climbing onto the mattress, he grabbed her ankles and pulled her toward him. "I like to start at the top and work my way down."

He began by dropping feather-light kisses on her eyelids and the tip of her nose. The contrast to his hot and heavy prelude in the hall had her hypersensitive. Caitlin shivered when he reached the hollow under her ear behind her jaw. "Go down faster."

She jerked when he nipped her lobe. "I'm not ready yet." Sean's hand trailed down her side until it reached her hip. Then he slipped his fingers over hers and into her panties, holding tight so they both rubbed her wet crease. "But you're ready for me, aren't you, Cait?"

Caitlin lost the ability to speak when he found her clit and squeezed. She tensed and Sean yanked her undies down her stiff legs. "Do I have your full attention now?" he asked. She could only nod, unable to trust her voice.

Sean leaned back to look at her. The loss of his touch made her skin ache. If he wasn't going to make a move, she'd have to. Caitlin trailed her fingers down his abs, counting in her head as she went. She reached the muscle above his hip and was about to follow it down, when he grabbed her hand.

"Patience." He climbed between the V of her legs,

pushing her knees out to the side. Finally, his dick nudged her opening and without warning, slid into her heat. She moaned as he stretched her out, the hard friction of his thrusting pushing her to a delicious edge. When his lips found her nipple and he pressed his tongue against it, she found her words.

"Holy fuck, Sean, don't stop."

She couldn't tell if he kept her on the brink by design or if she simply couldn't take that last step on her own, but when he finally shifted his mouth back to hers and palmed her breast, he sent her over. Caitlin curled, pressing into his chest, calling out to every saint and deity she could think of.

"My turn," Sean growled in her ear.

Caitlin wrapped a leg around his waist and moved with him as his breath came faster and faster. He didn't say a word as he jerked, pumping into her in a frenzy.

"Shit, Caitlin. You were worth the wait." He peeled a lock of sweat-damp hair from her cheek. He could be memorizing her face, he was staring at her so hard. It would only be fair; she'd memorized his. His green eyes had already been haunting her dreams for a while. Caitlin had a feeling she was wearing the same goofy smile he was. If he kept this up, her defenses wouldn't stand a chance against him.

Sean disappeared down the hall to the bathroom. When came back and pulled her under the sheets with him, he spooned her tight and sighed in her ear.

"The wait since last weekend?" she asked, thinking back to his previous statement.

His arms constricted around her ribs, guaranteeing her attention. "Are you telling me you didn't know I was interested since the moment I saw you?"

"Last year? At the volleyball tournament? You were

looking to bang anything that moved. No, I didn't think I was anything special to you."

"That's not fair."

"But it's true." She hadn't considered Sean as a remote possibility because of his reputation—not even after she caught him staring. Caitlin didn't mind casual, but she preferred the guy to not be out the door before the sheet fluttered back to the bed.

"Okay, it's true. I was younger and stupider then. The first time I saw you I thought you were gorgeous. Then you showed up on set and I was the one who got to work with you. We nailed every scene the very first day we worked together. That's when I knew we'd be a good fit. Then you refused to pay attention to me off set. I have never had to work this hard to get somebody into bed," he said.

"Good. Keep that in mind when you are wondering if something you're about to do is going to keep you out of my bed." The warning having been given, Caitlin tapped the back of the hand massaging her breast. "How are you feeling, stud? Did you want to order something in before we go again? You aren't a one-hit wonder, are you?"

"Cait, I can go all night with you. Keep in mind, if we order something now, we'll have time again before it gets here. Then we'll need to refuel. Then we can go for round three."

She had to love a man with that kind of stamina.

Chapter 9

SEAN didn't consider himself to be a shallow asshole. No, he had never considered a long-term commitment to any of his girlfriends in college, but he didn't treat the women he dated as disposable. He simply knew going in that the spark was going to burn itself out before he made any other kind of connection, so he didn't want to waste his time.

His spark with Caitlin, on the other hand, was unmissable. Yes, he'd been physically attracted to her at the beach, but he hadn't been able to get close to her at that time for a number of reasons. Chris was going after her friend, Sydney—and fucking it up royally—so Sean knew if lines were drawn, he'd be considered the enemy. There was also Caitlin's honorary big brother, a wounded vet named Trent Vaughn, who had threatened him if he so much as sniffed in her direction. Sean wasn't stupid enough to chase tail when the tail had a team of Navy bodyguards watching her back.

Then she joined Olympus and he was forced to keep it professional and treat her as a fellow actor. They worked together for a month and she wouldn't give him the time of day.

Looking back, her cool attitude was because of him. He'd barreled in, expecting what he usually got. It took him a while to understand Caitlin wasn't his usual interest. That realization made her more attractive. The longer it took for her to thaw, the hotter his engine revved for her.

Now that he had her, though, he had no idea what to do. He was twenty-seven years old. He hadn't expected to stop playing the field for a couple more years. The one thing he knew for sure was the chase had just begun. Every time he learned something new about Caitlin, two more questions popped up. His image of her was constantly changing and he was in awe of the view.

Sean supposed the first thing was to get another date now that they'd proven they were compatible in bed. It sucked he was fighting the reputation he'd been proud of. Now he had to convince Caitlin they weren't done. Not by a long shot.

So he was back to flowers. Not red roses, which he thought was a given. It turns out while they might be a classic thank you for a mind-blowing night full of orgasms, they could also say I didn't pay enough attention to find out what flowers you really like. Sean knew Caitlin liked pink and white, at least according to her bedspread and curtain. He asked the shop to put together something covering every shade of pink on the flower spectrum.

Thanks. Perfect. The tiny two-word text was worth the triple-digit bill.

Unfortunately, he didn't have time to gloat. A new PA—he knew the old ones by name—knocked on his trailer door. "Mr. Glenn, they need you on set ASAP."

It was the tone, not the words that got his attention. Worried, not impatient. Sean reached for his phone and raced out the set.

He grabbed the closest crewmember he could find when he saw the ambulance. "What happened?"

"Chris Peck collapsed on the set. They're taking him to the hospital."

This was very, very bad. Sean had seen Chris work

through a cold that left him voiceless. He hadn't missed a day after a fight-scene gone wrong left him with two cracked ribs. If he were going from the set to the hospital, he had to be dying.

"I can't reach Sydney."

The soft voice at his side startled him. "What?"

"I texted Syd to let her know what was going on. She hasn't called me back. I'll try her again." Caitlin's voice shook as she filled him in. "They were filming a Zeus and Hera scene. He didn't look good. He was sweating like crazy. The next thing I knew, he'd doubled over and hit the floor. Layla freaked the hell out."

Layla would. She did not handle illness well. Or blood. Or ambulances. Sean didn't know the whole story except the part where she had a deep-seated aversion to hospitals. Rumor had it she fainted when she tried to visit her boyfriend after he'd been injured on set in an accident involving one of Eros's misplaced arrows.

"Will Sydney need a ride to the hospital?" He had no idea if she'd fall apart at the news.

"No. She'll need help getting in to see him, though. She's not family and they aren't engaged yet."

"Yet?"

"I'm assuming Chris is going to do something on Valentine's Day. That's their anniversary. He'd better not die. That would mess Syd up permanently."

The ambulance rolled away, lights flashing. "Try her again. I'll talk to Layla and I'll see if I can find a way to let security know to keep an eye out for Sydney when she gets there." He didn't expect the crushing hug his words got him. Sean held tight until Caitlin was ready to let go. He glared at two different cast-mates who looked like they wanted to approach until they got the message he was occupied. When Caitlin let him go, she also allowed him to kiss her forehead. Sean may not want to be mobbed when he went out with Caitlin, but he wanted the world to know he had her.

He finally found Layla badly shaken. Her sister and assistant, Kristin, fed her two cans of full-sugar soda to stave off shock. "Chris has been feeling like crap all week," she told him. "Have you heard what's wrong with him?"

"He probably hasn't arrived at the hospital yet, Layla. Nobody knows anything yet."

"What about Sydney?" she asked.

"Caitlin's trying to reach her. I didn't think you two were friends," Sean said.

"We're not. She was nice when Russ got hurt, in a cursing-at-me-get-in-the-car kind of way. I'm not completely heartless." Sean shivered at the frost in her voice. He was impressed when he watched her shake off her ice-queen attitude. "Just, please keep me informed, okay?"

That woman was a complete mystery with the temper of an improperly wired firecracker fuse. Some days she had the patience of a saint; other days she went off with very little provocation. Sean fired off a quick text to her boyfriend, the show's former fight coordinator; to both warn him about Layla's state of mind, and to let him know about Chris. Russ Vukovich had been part of the crew for three years, and they still kept in contact now that he was working for his brother's company.

Then the worst part of the job kicked in. Even with a friend being rushed to the hospital, Sean couldn't stop to worry. The show must go on. Literally. At thousands of dollars an hour, they couldn't afford to shut down production when there were ways to work around Chris's sudden absence. They skipped ahead to a scene where Eros was arguing with the Greek goddess Athena about the upcoming war on Mount Olympus. Jennifer Jessica Smith held it together admirably, which flowed onto him, which he then carried into his next scene with Nick Thurston and Jason Ricker, who played Hephaestus. The final results could have been better, but considering the circumstances, nobody complained.

"They think it's his appendix. He's in surgery now," Caitlin told him during a quick break. "Syd is there. It's not good if it burst. Infections go bad very quickly." She didn't hang around long before she was called away to the hair and make-up trailer.

Sean wandered back to his trailer, scrolling through his contacts list to see who he could bother or bribe to get an update on Chris's condition

Martine was waiting for him. She waved her phone. "One thousand five hundred fifteen in less than thirty minutes. Not bad," she said.

Sean knew it was a set-up. He took the bait anyway. "One thousand five hundred fifteen what?"

"Likes on Benny's photo of you hugging Caitlin when you found out about Chris. Apparently your followers approve of Eros and Psyche as a couple in the real world."

"I know I approve."

The look she shot him gave him a shiver. "Sean, a word of advice from somebody who's seen this often. If you're serious about Caitlin, keep your relationship out of the press as much as you can. The public can turn on a dime and you don't want to get caught in the backlash. Fans like Eros and they like Psyche, and they even like Eros and Psyche together because of the whole star-crossed lovers thing. They don't like it when the real world messes with their fandom. Don't give them reason to get mad," she ordered.

"I'll talk with Caitlin about how she wants to handle it."

Going by the transformation of her stern frown to a beaming smile, that was exactly the right thing to say. He also had enough experience with women to know when to stop talking. He meant he'd ask Caitlin if she wanted to handle any future announcements or if he should deal with the social media.

His brain should have reminded his ego that dealing with women was never easy.

* * * *

"No," Caitlin said again after he asked her to repeat her answer. She'd ducked into his trailer to tell him dinner was off since Chris's appendix threw everyone's schedule into chaos. "No 'announcements' of any kind. My love life is not for public consumption. I'm not going to live my life in the media. That never ends well for anybody."

"You do realize that that is the definition of fame, don't you?"

"No, that's the definition of notoriety. Notoriety ends in drug addiction and leaked sex tapes and unemployment and death. I have no problem with talking about my job, but my private life is mine and nobody else's."

"Are you embarrassed to be seen with me? Why? In case this goes bad? If you aren't willing to try for a week, you should have said something before we made it into your bedroom. Your lack of faith pisses me off. Do you think I'm looking for my next hook-up? I have no intention of letting this go bad, Caitlin." He was beyond angry. He was tired of hearing the same excuses based on his past.

She stood quickly, making him take a step back unless he wanted her to bump his chest. The back of his knees hit his sofa and he sat down hard. Before he could move, Caitlin straddled his lap and took his face in her hands. "In addition to letting you know about dinner, I came here to ask if you were free for my movie premiere on Thursday. So, no, I'm not embarrassed to go out with you. What I'm saying is that going out with you and getting our pictures taken on the red carpet is one thing. Issuing updates to let people know how serious we are is something else. That is our business. Nobody else's. We can't stop them from speculating, but we don't have to feed the machine. Okay?"

His entire body was rock solid, and not in a good, sexy way from having Caitlin pressed against his cock. He was holding on to his temper with every ounce of control he had. He wasn't sure whom he was mad at anymore. Caitlin's stance made sense. After that understanding penetrated, it took a minute for his body to catch up to his brain. She dropped her hands to his shoulders and dug her fingers deep into his tense muscles until he relaxed. "Okay," he agreed.

"Is that a yes?"

"Yes to what?"

"Will you come to the premiere of Three Date Rule with me? Red carpet shenanigans. Free movie. Excellent secondary characters," she teased.

"Will I have to wear a tux?" he asked

"You don't have to, although I think you should know I'm absolutely helpless for a guy in a cummerbund." She dropped her hands to his waist and began playing with his belt buckle.

"Will you help me get dressed?"

A smile he was beginning to recognize spread across

her face. "I'll tell you what. Because we're both working the next day, I can either help you get dressed or…"

"Or what?"

"Or I can help you get undressed."

In that case…"I can get dressed on my own. I'm a big boy now."

Caitlin squirmed in his lap. "Yes you are." A walkie-talkie chirped outside the trailer door. "I have such lousy timing," she complained.

"Don't worry about it. You can make it up to me later," Sean said. Frankly, although his dick was ready and willing, his brain was exhausted. If he were taking Caitlin, he wanted more than mindless sex.

"Are we agreed? If asked, we'll say yes you are my date and 'no comment' to the rest?"

"No comment," Sean agreed.

* * * *

Caitlin took another selfie. It was for herself, mostly. She'd pick the best one of the sixteen she'd taken and post it before she left for her first movie premiere. Stressing the her. She'd attended one other movie premiere as somebody's date. This was her movie, for the ten minutes she was on screen. After a decade of auditioning, the idea of holding out for a leading role had been beaten out of her early on by utility bills. She'd take a decent small part in a big movie any day of the week. This time her character had a name, and lines, and was actually part of the plot instead of being part of the background. She didn't have the experience to know if that was enough to grant her access to the premiere. The invitation might have been Chris's doing; when the leading man asked for a small favor, people didn't say no.

Even better than the premiere, which was pretty fantastic in its own right, her four scenes had gotten her auditions for three more parts. She'd been turned down for two of them and was waiting to hear back from the third. She wouldn't be available for filming until the current Olympus season was over. That still left months she needed to fill with work. Years, if Psyche's storyline died an early death, which was likely. The show's human body count rivaled the one on Game of Thrones.

Caitlin took one last look in the mirror on the back of her bedroom door. She had taken Martine's advice to heart and went for sexy, not sex. Her dress was a true fuchsia—not red, not pink. If she photographed as well as she looked in her borrowed dress, she'd owe Vanessa Vaughn dinner. Her volleyball partner had performed miracles with pins and two-sided tape. Her friend had come over with her seamstress' kit and tailored the entire outfit to fit her like a very sexy glove. Caitlin added her own wide-strapped, silver heels, which gave her some height, but were comfortable enough to stand for hours. She'd also accented the dress with a thick, silver necklace and matching earrings.

After Sean arrived, he held her hand as he walked her down the stairs to the waiting limo. Damn, she was right. He looked fantastic in a tux. He was never going to be called pretty, though—he was too unmistakably male. There was something about him that hit all her buttons.

"You look incredible. Again." he said. "Are you ready to shine as Hollywood's newest rising star?"

She couldn't help it. She laughed. His corniness broke her stress and helped her remember tonight was supposed to be fun. "I'll remember you and the other little people when my name is at the top of the credits."

"Little, my ass," he growled in her ear, although he was careful not to mess up her hair.

Sean kept her distracted for most of the drive by

offering her snippets of advice on how to not get caught up by the photographers and how long she should hold a pose before moving on. He alternated by telling her various pieces of trivia of the Los Angeles landmarks they passed.

After she asked him to repeat himself for the third time, he laughed at her, and she realized he knew nothing he said was cutting through her excitement. He was simply trying to keep her from climbing the sides of the limousine until they arrived.

The theater was everything she'd imagined it would be. Fans, camera flashes, and an actual red carpet lining the sidewalk. Caitlin desperately wanted to take a picture, but she didn't want to come off as green as she actually was.

Sean—gloriously considerate Sean—made her pose outside the limo and took one for her. He took another of her standing on the carpet. "I know," was all he said as they posed for the first of the photographers.

They caused quite a stir among the reporters when she called Sean her date rather than her escort or friend.

Caitlin spotted a familiar, unexpected face along the ropes. "Mr. D! What a nice surprise. I didn't expect to see you here," she exclaimed. She'd met Gary Dobson and his wife when she'd gone with Sydney to visit her friend's grandmother. She'd beaten him at backgammon three games in a row before she figured out who he was. Sydney liked to tease her that Chris had recognized the retired, award-winning director before she'd finished their introduction.

"I wrangled an invitation. I couldn't let Sydney's fellow's film open without wishing him well." Gary Dobson shook his head sadly. "It's a shame they couldn't be here tonight. I understand he's doing better?"

Caitlin was grateful she could give him good news. "He's recovering nicely, but he's going to be out for a few more days."

"Mr. D, may I introduce Sean Glenn. Sean, this is Gary Dobson." She had to admit she was a little happy at the fact that it took Sean a full minute to realize with whom they were chatting. It made her feel less stupid about not knowing many people in the business yet.

The men were shaking hands when Caitlin felt a hand on the back of her arm. "Caitlin, you look lovely," Robert Clancy said, loud enough to carry. "Keep smiling. We need you to press some flesh as one of the faces for Three Day Rule," he whispered.

People did not say no to Robert if they ever wanted to work in film again. Caitlin didn't hesitate before nodding in agreement. Nothing about this made sense. "Why me?" she whispered between smiling lips.

"You're all we've got."

"What?"

Robert excused them, leaving Sean standing there with a somewhat bewildered look on his face. Mr. Dobson nodded at her and Robert, then at Sean. "Don't worry, Gary will fill him in," Robert said as he ushered them down the carpet as quickly as he could. "We split the cast between L.A. and New York for the premieres. We were supposed to have Lissa Pratt and Chris here, as well as Corinne and Connor Gately."

Caitlin knew those names. Chris and Lissa were the movie's leads. Corinne and Connor were the story's antagonists, playing the leads' evil exes. In an interesting twist, they were also brother and sister and they were insanely funny on and off camera. "Where are they?" she asked.

"Chris is just out of the hospital, Lissa has the

fucking chicken pox of all things, Corinne broke her leg on a ski trip yesterday, and Connor called two hours ago. He's in gridlock on PCH because of an accident. He doesn't know when he'll get here. You're it."

"You didn't fly anybody back from New York?" There was the hero and heroine's best friends, and Audrey McLean, the multi-Oscar winner who played Chris's boss, and—

"We have two actors sitting on a runway in Denver because their plane had mechanical problems. Caitlin, there is nobody else. You are it. Can you do this or not?" Robert demanded.

Her back stiffened automatically at his tone. She'd grown up with a military command voice like that. "Of course, I can do it. Where do I start?" She knew what to do in theory. Putting it into practice without any kind of rehearsal or script had her doubting herself. She set aside the fear. Caitlin smiled and posed for cameras and answered questions, greeting every reporter she recognized from TV by name. She caught Sean's eye for a quick minute, and he offered her a strange smile before she had to dive back in.

It. Was. Awesome.

By the time they had to move inside, Caitlin's face hurt from smiling. She latched onto Sean's arm and let him lead her into the theater. Despite her adrenaline high, she could sense his tension. "What's wrong?"

"Nothing. Let's enjoy the movie."

His nothing was definitely something, but she didn't have time to ask more before the lights dimmed. Caitlin settled in to watch the show.

Chapter 10

SEAN didn't know which was worse: the fact that Caitlin felt bad about deserting him on the red carpet after discovering she had to work during what was supposed to be a big date for them, or what happened after she left. She hadn't precisely ignored him on the red carpet. She checked on him every few minutes. It wasn't like she forgot he was there. He couldn't say she'd abandoned him either; she'd left him with Gary Dobson. The old man had been interesting and had introduced him to a handful of movers and shakers he wouldn't have met otherwise.

He didn't even mind the hit to his ego because Caitlin was so excited. After three years on Olympus, he was used to being a big name at various events, which is why he didn't blink the first few times he heard "Olympus star Sean Glenn and his date Caitlin Kelly" coming from the sidelines. After Robert Clancy grabbed her, he was downgraded to "Olympus actors Sean Glenn and Caitlin Kelly." By the time they finished on the red carpet, he'd been reduced to "Three Date Rule's Caitlin Kelly and her date, Sean Glenn." He had to admit, the downgrade burned a bit, although that wasn't it either.

He knew Caitlin was looking at him funny as they made their way to their seats. He didn't say anything, not wanting to spoil her big night. Unfortunately, it looked like he did just that. She apologized again for leaving him, but the lights dimmed before he could explain what had happened to sour his mood.

When Gary Dobson had finished his introductions, Sean moved up the carpet to keep pace with Caitlin. A gaggle of teenaged Olympus fans drew him to the ropes where he took several selfies with them before he noticed the brunette beside them.

After endless nagging from Caitlin and much hounding from Martine, he eventually did file a report about the woman who had jumped him at the charity dinner. He couldn't do anything about it after the fact except get the incident on record. The process did provide him with one important piece of information: the woman's name. Shannon Tolliver. The woman he called exuberant and harmless had no criminal record except one harassment complaint filed against her by another actor, which was later dropped. She was no threat at all. Sean didn't tell the bossy women in his life they had over-reacted, but only because he liked his balls attached.

Then he had seen Shannon Tolliver again at the restaurant when he and Caitlin were on their second date. Or he thought he did. There was no sign of her after his quick spin around the block. He chalked it up to contagious paranoia.

But now she was here. At Caitlin's premiere. All of a sudden, he felt he hadn't been nearly paranoid enough. Shannon offered her phone in invitation like he'd taken a handful of others. With an icy knot in the pit of his stomach, he turned away like he hadn't seen her, and crossed to the other side of the carpet.

He was so busy avoiding that potential threat, he walked into another one. Megan was there, on the red carpet, with fuck-knows-who. She was quick to abandon her date and attach herself to his arm. "I'm sorry if I got you in trouble with the little lady. Why don't you invite Caitlin to join us next time? We can teach her the score?

We both know she's not going to be able to hold you on her own. She might as well learn how to share from the get-go," she added with a smirk. "Or, if you prefer, the two of us can sneak away during the movie and find a quiet spot to finish what we started the other day."

There were cameras around. Fortunately they weren't close enough to hear what she was saying. He blinked at the gorilla who was stomping over to them. He mustered a smile and made his position clear. "There is no us. It's done. Stay away from me, Megan. Stay away from Caitlin."

"No. We're not done," Megan insisted.

He shrugged her off and spun her into the gorilla's arms. Her date looked pissed but Sean was angrier. "You two should head inside now," he said. It wasn't a suggestion. The other guy knew it.

Sean hadn't been able to get Caitlin inside and out of sight fast enough. Now he was half an hour into a movie and he had no idea what was happening because he hadn't been paying attention. He was too busy trying to figure out what to do about his new shadows.

Caitlin derailed his line of thought completely when she dug her nails into his arm. She leaned forward in her seat, as if it would give her a better look at the screen. "What?" he whispered harshly, biting back a very undignified whimper.

"Listen!"

Sean concentrated on the movie. He didn't understand what had caught her attention. She wasn't in the scene. Caitlin collapsed into her chair and whispered at him again. "Oh my God!" This time she did look at him and the glow on her face was even greater than it had been outside. She nudged him until he caught the hint. He lifted his arm and wrapped it around her shoulders. "I'll tell you later," she promised.

If it weren't Chris and Caitlin's movie, he never would have come. Two hours of romantic comedy stretched his patience to his absolute limit. The only reasons he lasted through the entire thing was to be supportive, and because he couldn't piss off Caitlin before she helped him out of his tuxedo. He could tolerate a little saccharine-sweet dialogue for that.

She made him stay seated until the very last frame of the movie. Near the end of them, when the music credit rolled, she gripped his forearm again. "Caitlin, what's going on?" he asked.

"Look!"

He glanced back to the screen and caught sight of her name before it rolled out of view. "What was that?"

"Motive for murder," Caitlin said.

"What!"

"Come on, places to go, people to kill, tuxedos to remove," she sang, pulling him to his feet.

Of course, it wasn't that simple. "You know, we could skip the middle step and save some time," Sean suggested.

"No. It'll be fun!" she promised. Caitlin dragged him into the lobby and searched the crowd until she spotted who she was looking for. "Let's go say hello to the boys."

Sean took his own turn scanning the room. When he didn't spot Shannon or Megan, his chest loosened a little. His tension eased more when he saw the boys Caitlin referred to. The rest of Charlie Oscar Echo had also gotten into the premiere. "What are they doing here?" he asked.

"Dying. Slowly." They approached the trio, Caitlin smiling broadly. "Gentlemen," she said.

They tried to smile. Bobby Wheaton managed a sincere one. "Hi, Caitlin. Great movie! You were awesome," he said.

Caitlin studied him carefully, like a smile under a microscope. "You didn't know."

Bobby shook his head. "Nope. I'm glad you and I left the books to Greg and Peter and took up the marketing and book side of the business instead. They're completely responsible for our current contracts, including with Retro Sound."

Pieces began to fall into place. "Wasn't Retro Sound the name of the company who produced the soundtrack? You pointed out their name in the credits," Sean said.

"It is."

"Wasn't Charlie Oscar Echo also in the credits?" Sean asked.

"It was," Caitlin agreed.

"And you knew nothing about this?"

"Not a thing. Although it does explain why Watching Him Watching Her suddenly became our second release. I assume you released the video already?"

Peter nodded frantically. "It's good. Honest. We sent you copies of the paperwork as soon as the film ended. It's in your mailbox."

"And we paid you your share. Your shares. We just held onto it for a little while in the band's account to surprise you," Greg added, looking at Bobby. "Surprise?"

"No wonder murder is on the menu." Sean laughed at the sheer audacity of Caitlin's friends. This was awesome. It was huge. Starring in—well not starring— being in a movie and having a song on the soundtrack would be incredible for her career. Especially with the press she'd be getting from tonight.

"We will be discussing this during the weekend,"

Caitlin said, shaking her finger at each of them. "In detail. With hard copies of the contract," she specified. "But for now, Sean and I are going home. We have to work tomorrow."

"Like you're going to be in any shape to work tomorrow," Bobby said, leering at her cleavage while he pretended to drool.

Caitlin looked over her shoulder at the emptying lobby, then lunged at the drummer. She grabbed his nipple through the navy dress shirt he wore and gave it a violent twist.

"I'm sorry! No more comments about Caitlin's love life," Bobby promised as he rubbed his chest.

"Her very acti—" She whirled on Peter, who slapped his arms across his chest. "Not a word," Peter said.

Sean made sure the buttons of his jacket were fastened and Greg stepped out of reach.

"You guys are such assholes. See you in a couple days. Send me links for everything," she ordered before she let Sean walk her out of the theater.

Sean felt much more comfortable knowing the true status of Caitlin's relationship with the band after witnessing it firsthand. They weren't ex-boyfriends. They were brothers. From the looks they gave him when they found out he was taking her home, very protective big brothers who would not hesitate to beat him to a pulp if he hurt Caitlin. He could take two of them, but Greg gave him pause. Sean didn't want to mess with him.

Caitlin collapsed on the limo's bench seat. Her neck lolled bonelessly against the headrest. "That was incredible. And now I'm dead. I'm glad we have a late call time tomorrow." She moaned, then kicked off her outrageously high heels and let them fall to the floor.

Sean grabbed her ankle and pulled it into his lap. He

dug his thumb into the arch of her foot and watched in satisfaction as a shiver wracked her entire body. He found a spot that made her groan at almost the same pitch as when he slipped his hand into her panties and found a particularly sensitive spot. Encouraged, he trailed his fingers over her ankle, up her calf, and past her knee. "I sense a revival coming on," he said.

* * * *

The only second Caitlin wasted was when she stepped through Sean's front door and the zipper under her arm got caught on a loose thread. She yanked hard and broke it, then made a mental note to check it for damage in the morning.

She circled Sean, her skin covered in goose bumps because of the air-conditioning in his bedroom, which was set much too high. Her dress was in his dining room, tossed over the back of one of the chairs as they made their way upstairs. The pearl-pink bra and panties set offered her little protection from the cold. Sean hadn't even removed his jacket. "Aren't you coming to bed?"

He shook his head. "You promised to undress me."

If that's how he wanted to play it, she was game. It didn't mean she was going to make it easy for him. Caitlin snuggled against his back and wrapped her arms around his waist. Her breasts pushed against the satiny black material. With her heels on, her chin touched Sean's shoulder at just the right height to whisper in his ear. She undid the buttons on his jacket one at a time, and stepped back. She eased it over his shoulders and stepped forward again, undoing his tie and pulling it out from under his collar. Her next move was to take hold of his belt buckle. Sean covered her hand. "I think you're rushing things a bit, Cait."

She nipped his ear. "Don't be ridiculous. I know how

long shirttails are. I can't take off your shirt 'til your pants are down." Caitlin slipped her hand under his belt and cupped the bulge behind his zipper. "Don't you want to get this out of your pants and into something else?"

"You are a tease, Cait," Sean said. His voice was rough and he trembled under her hands. She liked that.

"No, I'm not. A tease would leave you hanging. I intend to follow through." She tugged his belt free of the loops and dropped it at his feet. His unbuttoned fly fell open, but his slacks stayed on his hips until she began tugging the white shirt over the waistband. That's when he snapped.

It took him long enough.

Sean ripped his shirt over his head and tossed it behind him. His pants hit the floor a second later and he balanced on one foot to toe off his shoes even as he lifted her up. "Time to follow through."

Thank. God. Caitlin could play the seductive siren to get a man into the bedroom. But it was much more fun once she got to the main event. Especially if the guy knew what he was doing. Sean knew plenty.

She blinked and her underwear was gone. Vanished. She hadn't felt them go. Sean hooked his finger under her bra strap and nodded in approval. Before she could blink again, it was gone too, and she was naked against sheets that felt like heaven. Then Sean was on her. Under her. In her.

It was more than a kiss. His tongue demanded entry to her mouth. When she let him in, he stole her breath. His lips were hot and hard and hungry. He wanted to feast on her and she gladly let him. Every part of her that touched part of him burned.

Finally, finally, he wedged his thigh between hers and parted her knees. His calloused fingers rubbed the sensitive bare skin leading to the V between her legs. He gave her clit the gentlest caress and froze. Just stopped.

"What's wrong?" she whispered. Whispered because her throat was too tight to speak normally.

"I'm waiting for an air horn or something," he teased.

Caitlin loved a man who could joke in bed. But not right now. "No air horns. I promise a choir of singing angels if you move a little to the left," she promised.

He complied and all of a sudden she was wrapped around two of his fingers. "Love that," she gasped. She arched her back to press against his hand. He stopped her, leaning to hold her against the mattress.

"We'll get there, Cait." His hand did all kinds of exploring until she came on his fingers, straining under him on the bed. Sean kissed her slowly as she came back down. "Did that take the edge off?" he asked.

She couldn't have stood if she tried. She was barely able to lie there and remember to breathe at the same time. "Barely."

"I can fix that."

Then he was there, filling her more with each stroke. Caitlin fisted the sheets as he moved, brushing a discarded condom wrapper on the floor in her desperate scramble to find an anchor from the sensations swamping her. His cock between her legs, his palm on her breast, his mouth at her neck…There was nothing outside of her connection to Sean. A forever later and still too soon, his rhythm faltered and he shuddered as he spilled into her.

Sean kissed her again. "Thank you, Cait." He shifted off her, and, to her surprise, lifted her in his arms and carried her to the bathroom. They cleaned up in silence until he took her hand and led her back to his bed. She wanted to say something, anything, but exhaustion hit her as soon as he pulled the blankets over them. "Good night, Cait."

"Night, Sean. Thank you."

"Absolutely, anytime."

Chapter 11

HE could get used to waking with Caitlin in his bed on a permanent basis. She gave him soft and sweet in the evening and fast and furious in the morning. While Sean could remember more extreme lovers he'd taken, he could no longer say he'd had better. He was straight-out happy.

Like earlier, when she said he made the earth move for her, when really a minor earthquake woke the entire San Fernando Valley and surrounding area. Or like now, when she was freaking out in the bathroom because she'd forgotten to pack her shampoo and she had to use his which, "smells as harsh as Irish Spring, and do you know how damaging that is to a person's follicles?"

He laughed when she told him she could drink a cup of coffee in the shower. He laughed harder when she went on to prove it. Caitlin was fun and unpredictable and totally sure of herself. He wasn't used to the combination.

She was also the most organized, driven person of either sex he'd ever met in his life. Caitlin was waiting for him in his kitchen when he finally made it downstairs. Despite the obscenely early hour, especially after the lateness of the night before, she was on her phone talking business. Finishing business, by the sounds of it.

"It's a good thing you know how to negotiate, Greg. It sounds fine. I'll need to see it on paper. Do you have my fax number?" She blew Sean a kiss and continued her conversation. "Sounds great. Thank you."

He waited until she hung up before he asked, "Fax?"

Caitlin nodded. "It's my dad's fault. He insists contracts be paper-based for future legal reference because computer hackers can change on-line documents."

"What does your dad do? All I know is he's in the military."

"He was an M.P. Military Police."

"Wow, you must not have gotten away with anything as a kid." His dad was a rancher with a wicked sense of humor that drove his mother nuts. If there was trouble to find on the property, his dad was the one leading the way.

"That's why we started the band. Our parents knew where we were and what we were doing. As long as noise was coming out of the garage, they didn't bother to keep an eye on us."

"And what did you do in those garages?" Sean asked.

"I'd like to tell you we practiced hotwiring cars or something, but mostly we played and plotted how we were going to get the hell out of our parents' houses after graduation. Although there was one summer at a base in Texas when I taught the guys how to two-step and waltz to impress the girls at our school dances. They were fast learners. After that, I spent the rest of the years getting paid for giving dance lessons to other guys from my school. Some of the girls too. I bought my first truck with my dance class money. My dad hated it."

"I'll have to put my skills against theirs to see if you were a better teacher than my mom," Sean said.

"I've seen you dance. We should make it a bet," Caitlin suggested.

"What do I get if I win?" Sean asked.

"Me."

"And if I lose?"

"Still me. You'll also have to take me dancing so you can practice," Caitlin said.

"You're on. As soon as we can set it up." He didn't know if he wanted to win or lose.

"We've got to get going." Caitlin put away her phone—put it away as in turned it off, to give him her full attention. Sean loved it; he did the same. Going cell-free was something he seldom did. He lasted eight minutes; long enough for Caitlin to grab her overnight bag, get into his recently returned car, and back down the driveway. He made it halfway to the street before he slammed on the brakes at Caitlin's horrified gasp.

"What the fuck is that?" Caitlin asked.

Sean hit the brakes. "Did I hit something?"

"No. Look." She pointed at the now-closed garage door. It was covered in graffiti which spread across his house to his front door. "Cunt" and "Cheater" were the most common insults, but he couldn't read some of it where the vandal had apparently lobbed the entire contents of an open paint can at the exterior brick wall.

"Motherfucker." Some dipshit little weasel thought they could come to my house while I was asleep and do that? While Caitlin was there? In a split second, he thought of a dozen ways he was going to tear the community's private security company a new asshole.

"I have an earlier set call time than you. I can call Ash," Caitlin said. "She doesn't start work 'til eleven. She can come get me and take me back to my place to grab my truck. I can get myself to the studio while you deal with this."

No. He did not want her going off on her own. Not when there was a nutcase on the loose targeting him. Or possibly her. It wasn't safe. If he was the target, Caitlin would be better off far away from him. "I'm really sorry. I think you should call Ashleigh."

She offered him a smile with the slightest tinge of tears to it. "We almost had an entire date go well. We set a new record at any rate."

"I guess we'll have to try again until we get it right."

* * * *

He made it to the studio in time for his first scene, although it was a near thing. By the time Ashleigh picked up Caitlin, the police were already on scene, as well as a posse of incompetent security guards who swore they had no idea how his house got trashed in full view of the street, despite a gated entrance to the community and roving patrols.

Sean was tempted to let it drop. Turpentine and a fresh coat of paint could make it look like nothing ever happened. But something had happened. Somebody had avoided his house alarm and literally walked to his front door. While Caitlin was under his roof. That was unacceptable.

The cops gave him shit about not reporting the vandalism on his car. It was unnecessary since he was already kicking his own ass. He couldn't prove the same person had gone after him twice, although the likelihood he was involved in two unrelated incidents in a month were miniscule. He answered every question truthfully. Then they asked if he have any enemies.

It was fucking embarrassing. The first two people who popped to mind were women half his size who had never said a threatening word to him. A fan with bad judgment and an ex-girlfriend with a bad attitude. He had nothing to fear if he came face-to-face with either of them. He could take care of himself. But.

But these weren't frontal attacks. He couldn't stop

what he couldn't see. More importantly, he couldn't protect Caitlin from what he couldn't see. He could either continue as he'd been doing, cleaning up messes that were pains in his ass, but not real threats yet, or he could be proactive and potentially put innocent people under an uncomfortable microscope to protect both himself and his woman.

"Megan Unger and Shannon Tolliver," he said. "That's where I'd start. I don't know Shannon. I can warn you Megan is not going to cooperate." He told them about the charity banquet, and the restaurant, and the premiere. Their frowns grew at each incident. By the time he finished, he had an appointment with a detective arranged for later that day, as well as half a dozen recommendations for private security firms to upgrade his current system and offer personal protection.

As bad as it had been, Sean would have happily stayed there and dealt with the police and security and insurance people all day long. Anything would be better than having the same conversation with Caitlin later. She was going to kick his ass for keeping her in the dark.

* * * *

Caitlin felt herself falling and braced for an intimate introduction to the concrete soundstage floor. She didn't notice the approaching shadow until she jerked to a stop inches from the ground. Mike Mosley tightened the grip he had on her waist and held tight until she was upright again. "Are you okay?" he asked.

She kicked at the cord that had wrapped itself around her foot during the aftershock. When she was finally free, she nodded. "Thanks. I'm a little distracted. Good catch."

"No problem. We're already down Chris and Jessica. We can't afford to lose anybody else."

"Wait? What happened to Jess?" Her friends were

dropping like flies.

"Bruised ribs," Mike said.

At this rate, they were going to have to shut down production due to lack of actors. "Are you kidding me? When did this happen?"

"You didn't hear? A wall on Hephaestus's set fell over during the mini-quake this morning. You have rewrites in your trailer. The writers are going insane trying to keep up. They congratulated us for moving up the call sheet one body at a time."

Jessica was going to be out for days, maybe a week. That meant one episode, if not more. Chris was out for at least one. Caitlin remembered a toast she'd heard from a British soldier who'd visited her dad once and had talked about getting a promotion. The toast he gave was "To a bloody war or a sickly season." It referred to the two ways you didn't want to advance in the ranks. Mike's joke had the same dark undertones. Everybody wanted more screen time, but not at the expense of their cast-mates' health.

"You know I wasn't the first choice for Psyche, right? The original actress was in a car accident a week before they started filming."

"That's okay. I wasn't the original Dionysus either. Come on. Let's take a break." Mike led her to a quiet strip of sunshine outside the sound stage. "This is not how I imagined my career taking off. I mean, everybody jokes they'd kill for a role, but shit."

Caitlin knew what he meant. "Yeah. Did you hear about last night? I got to meet the press because Lissa Pratt has the chicken pox. Corinne Gately broke her leg. I'm starting to get a complex about auditioning for anything. Thank God two of the last three projects I auditioned for have already wrapped."

"And the third?" he asked.

"I didn't get it. They announced casting." If she were honest with herself, it was almost as big a relief as it was a disappointment. It would be a bigger movie role than she'd ever done before—the second female lead—but with the show, the band, and her current luck, it might be better for all involved for her to wait for the next one.

Mike stared at her for a full minute before speaking again. "Nobody knows yet. I got the Nikolai campaign. The model they originally hired OD'ed last week. He didn't make it."

"Oh!" She couldn't say "oh, congrats!" A man was dead. It was a horrible way to step into a massive men's cologne advertising campaign, no matter how big an opportunity it was.

"I know. Believe me, I know."

"At least we should be safe from each other, right? Provided we don't compete for the same roles."

His mood broke. His deep laugh erupted and triggered her own giggle fit. "How about we keep each other informed when we go out for other jobs?" Mike suggested. "It'll give us a chance to put on our Kevlar underwear, just in case."

"That sounds like an excellent plan. In the meantime, I need a drink," Caitlin said.

"How about new pages instead?"

"Fine. But if Psyche kills or maims a single god or mortal, I'm refusing to come out of my trailer."

Maybe she was imagining things. People on set seemed to be staying away from her. Erin, the show's hairdresser, practically chased her out of the trailer as if she were contagious when Layla arrived. Her paranoia hit new heights when she received a call later that afternoon. Then she hit new lows when she couldn't reach Sean to share her news. It seemed he was avoiding her. Caitlin shrugged it off, giving nobody watching any clue as to how upset she was at being abandoned.

Wanting to fall apart in private, she ran for her trailer. She veered off at the last second where she spotted another safe spot. She took the skin off her knuckle banging on Mike's door. "Please be here," she muttered to herself.

He opened the door wrapped in a towel. Streams of water running down his chest briefly distracted her from what she wanted to say. They reminded her of tears and Caitlin found herself on the verge of crying again.

Mike wrapped an arm around her shoulders and ushered her into his trailer. He gave her a gentle shove toward the sitting area. "Be right back." He came back in camo pants and a white T-shirt which had gone transparent in the wet spots. "Who died?" he asked.

"Kara Truscott." Caitlin didn't know why she was crying. She'd never met the woman. She'd never seen her in anything. And she was absolutely not responsible for her suicide.

Mike shook his head, evidently also unfamiliar with the name. Then he connected the dots and sighed. "So they offered you the part after all?"

She sniffled and nodded. "Yay, me." Caitlin leaned into him when he sat beside her. "Aren't we a pair?" she asked.

"I thought we were a pair," a familiar voice said from the door. "What am I looking at, Cait?"

Caitlin looked up to see Sean glaring down at them. She didn't shift away from Mike, or shrug his arm off her shoulder. He was a friend who'd been there for her when Sean couldn't be bothered to return a text. It wasn't like they'd done anything wrong.

"Ease off, Glenn. She's had a bad day," Mike warned him.

"So have I," Sean growled. "This scene isn't helping."

"Did anybody die?"

Sean's eyes widened. "No."

"Caitlin wins," Mike said.

"Died? Really?" His voice trailed off and he looked to Mike for confirmation. "Who?"

"Kara Truscott."

"Honey, you must be devastated," Sean said.

She snorted. "You have no idea." Sean didn't say anything else. If he had opened his mouth at that point, she would have shut it for him. Caitlin didn't comment when Mike moved and Sean took his place. She shrugged to let him know she didn't want his arm around her shoulders. He didn't move. She sniffled again. There was nothing left for her to say.

Chapter 12

BODIES trumped vandalism and potential stalkers. If Sean could have cut out his own tongue, he would have. Yes, it looked bad when he walked in on Mike with his arm around Caitlin, but if he'd held his temper for a fraction of a second, he would have noticed the tear tracks on her cheeks and not made the situation worse.

It was a good thing he'd talked to her about spending the night at her place while his insurance company arranged for clean-up. He didn't think he would have gotten in the door otherwise. "Why don't you have a bath or a shower or whatever you like while I wait for the food to get here?" he suggested.

Caitlin retreated to her bedroom and Sean waited to hear the water running. Bath. He hadn't been sure which way she'd go. There was so much they didn't know about each other. It was obvious they were compatible in bed, but he was clueless on the little, intimate things, like whether she preferred to have a bath or a shower when she was upset. Or how she was prepared to deal with a stalker who was vaulting over steps on the violence scale.

He waited for the water to stop flowing and the splashing to slow down before he started to breathe easier. He followed a loud male voice into the corridor. Marcus was at the end of the hall, staring out the window over the parking lot in the back. His hair was pulled up in a man-bun to keep it out of his face as he gave instructions on a cell-phone. "If I'm wiring Glenn's place tonight, I'll need somebody to cover my shift tomorrow with the singer chick from Seattle. Yeah, he'll do. I'll call later with an update."

"Do you think you'll get my place done in one night?" Sean asked.

"What? Is there something wrong with the babe's bedroom? Not enough sound proofing?"

Motherfucker, Caitlin was right. This guy was an asshole. Just because Sean hired his company to redesign his security system didn't mean he could—

"Fuck, man, sorry. You're a client now. I'm so used to giving Cait's guys a hard time it's a habit," Marcus said.

"Does she have a lot of guys you need to be a dick to?" Sean asked.

"Speaking of dick maneuvers," Marcus shot back, "client or not, that question is out of line. Yes, your house should be finished by tomorrow. Anyway, you're covered here for tonight or as long as you need. Ashleigh's getting a quality system installed throughout the building, but it's going to take a few days. We have temporary cameras watching the parking lot until it's done."

Sean didn't want to apologize. "Thanks." He'd played the jealousy card once today and Caitlin rightly called a foul. If he did it again, he had no doubt she'd toss him from the game.

Marcus gave him a nod. "It's good you're taking this seriously. Women generally do. Guys tend to blow it off until it's too late. We've got you covered. Do you want me to explain the new procedures to Caitlin?"

"No, I've got it. Listen, I've got to get back. If anything happens at my place—"

"If anything happens, we'll deal with it. You sleep easy."

"Thanks."

"Or don't sleep."

"Bolling," Sean growled in warning.

"Fine, Mr. Client. I apologize. Shit, you have no sense of humor. If Caitlin has questions, call me."

Caitlin would not be calling Marcus for any reason. It was bad enough she saw the graffiti in the first place. Sean wasn't going to pile on bad news, especially after learning her friend had died. He could deal with everything and keep the stress off her.

He had the delivered Chinese food on plates by the time Caitlin wandered back into the living room, bundled in a baby-blue knee-length terry robe. She managed to eat half of what he gave her before putting her plate down.

"Crappy day, huh? I'm sorry about your friend," he said.

"My friend? Shit, what happened now?"

"Kara. Your friend who died"

"She wasn't my friend. I never met her. I have no idea who she is." Her tears started again and he was lost.

That was it. Sean hauled her into his lap, narrowly avoiding knocking their plates off the coffee table. "Talk to me, Cait. I can't help you if I don't know what's going on."

"It's a long story."

"I have time."

"It's a horrible story," she said, squirming. Sean held her tighter.

"You aren't running me off. Talk," he ordered.

So she talked. He listened. He tensed a couple times, but he didn't bolt. By the time Caitlin finished her litany of people who had fallen along the wayside during the rise of her acting career, he completely understood her fears she was cursed. "Oh, honey, that's awful luck."

"Right? Do I call them back and say I can't take the

role?"

"Fuck, no. You do the job."

"Don't you think it'll make me look like a vampire? Or vulture? Or some other monster that benefits from corpses and violent accidents?"

Sean was out of his depth. He didn't have a ton of experience in the industry, but he'd never heard of anybody with Caitlin's history of stepping into roles. Or another actor with her body count. She was lying in his arms and if he were honest about it, he was glad he'd never had to go up against her for a part. The thought was completely unfair since none of what happened was even remotely Caitlin's fault. She just had spectacularly good timing—or bad, depending on which side of the event you were on. "Not at all." Providing nobody else knew. "You've got to go for it, and keep going for it. It's your career. None of those incidents"—many, many incidents—"are your fault or responsibility. You should keep on, no matter what else comes up."

Caitlin let out the most heartfelt, heartbreaking sigh he'd ever heard on or off camera. She melted into him. Considering the other shit swirling in his life, the fact he'd made her feel good about something and had taken some weight off her shoulders had him on top of the world. She did that to him.

"Thank you."

"Any time," he whispered back.

"I'll text my agent and tell her to go ahead and schedule my next audition."

"You have another audition?"

"How else am I going to be the number one box office draw on the planet five years from now if I stop auditioning?" Caitlin asked. While her tone was teasing, Sean heard the truth behind it.

"That's your dream?"

"No, that's my future."

"Aren't you busy enough? The show, Charlie Oscar Echo, a movie during hiatus two years running? You're going to burn yourself out." His concern for her health was legitimate. It was also the only thing he could see going wrong for her. Caitlin had the drive, and the talent to match. When he thought about the amount of hustle she put out, he felt like a slacker in comparison. He enjoyed Olympus and he was putting some money away. He wasn't worried about not having any plans beyond the show. When it ended there would be another one. He didn't have a five-year plan in play, let alone had any items crossed off it. He was happy just acting and enjoying the ride.

"I figure the show has two more seasons after this one, tops. If Psyche survives," Caitlin said. "If that happens, I can concentrate on movies while I look for a new show. Charlie and the guys are a lot of fun, but I never thought the band would get anywhere near the amount of attention we're getting. Don't get me wrong, I love it. I just didn't expect it. It's adding variables and confusing my options."

"Speaking of options, what do you say we move off the sofa to your bed?" Caitlin was a puddle against him. Her muscles were slack under his hands as he stroked her arms and back. She was barely awake. Despite the early hour, the predawn start and the late night before were taking their toll. She was in no shape to have a conversation about Sean's maybe-stalker or about the new security procedures he put in place. There'd be time to talk in the morning when they were both awake. In the meantime, they had a bodyguard outside the door. Sean had time.

* * * *

He was still there. In her bed. Caitlin lay still, and marveled at the man snoring beside her. She hadn't chased him off. Sean had a lot of things working in his favor. He was good-looking, smart, and hard working. He also tended to be late, felt the need to overcompensate with his car, and talked much more than he had to about basketball. She could work around those things. Most importantly, tonight he hadn't freaked out when she told him she had a five-year career plan. He hadn't made fun of her either. Caitlin tried to remember the last time a man took her seriously when she mentioned it. She couldn't think of one. Sean was the first to not only take her at her word, but encourage her. She was keeping him.

The next morning at the studio she decided she was keeping Martine Peeples as well. She let the blonde into her trailer when she arrived and Martine made herself at home. "You had quite the premiere the other night," Martine said.

"I did," Caitlin agreed. "It was unexpected."

"You impressed a lot of people," Martine continued. "There and at the charity function with Jay Wilson. You're getting quite the reputation as a reliable go-to person when the shit hits the fan."

"Thank you." Caitlin was missing something. She wasn't sure what it was, but she knew it was big. The studio's top PR person would not drop by to give her compliments.

Martine stared at her for a moment before she burst into laughter. "You are too cute. Unfortunately, I'm here to tell you that you can't afford to be cute anymore."

"What? Why?" Cute was working for her. Cute had accomplished great things in the last year. Besides, wasn't Martine the one who said sexy, not sex? Caitlin had the cute and sexy thing down.

"You have an agent, right?" Martine asked.

"Of course I have an agent."

"How about a publicist? Or a manager?"

Caitlin had neither. She couldn't afford them. If her agent hadn't been getting her small, steady jobs, she wouldn't have been able to afford him either. She shrugged, and Martine took her response for what it was.

"This is beyond the scope of my official responsibilities, Caitlin, but I strongly suggest you get one, the other, or both. Talk to some of the people here for recommendations. You've done great handling everything on your own, but you have to know you're going to need the help sooner rather than later. If you have someone in place, you won't miss any opportunities."

Caitlin must have made a face because Martine kept talking. "You have more opportunities, don't you?" Martine asked with a sigh.

"Not officially?" Caitlin hedged. Shit. She ought to tell Martine about her upcoming role. Superstition held her back. Until the contract was signed, she didn't want to breathe a word. And, to be honest with herself, she didn't want to advertise the fact that yet another actress had gone down to allow her to step up.

"When it is official, let me know. Caitlin, this is the big time. You've been called up from the minors. It's time to let everybody know you are here to stay. I've been on hand when other actors have had the chance to take off like you are, and the ones who seized the opportunity have never looked back. I can't tell you what to do. I hope you'd take my advice, though."

Caitlin got the hint, loud and clear. Martine was talking bigger than Chris Peck, who was no slouch when it came to making the leap to the big screen. She was talking Will Smith, Dwayne Johnson, or Mark Wahlburg levels of dominating in more than one entertainment genre. Caitlin could totally do that.

"And, since the movie's soundtrack is getting a lot of play, I'm pretty sure you are announcing your presence all over the place. It's time to step up," she advised kindly.

"I'll ask around," Caitlin promised. She'd been wondering if it was time to invest in her future, now that she had a little cash coming in. Apparently it was.

"Congratulations for your song. I hear the soundtrack is poised to crack the top one hundred when the next Billboard list comes out."

"Thank you. I've heard those rumors. It's great." Caitlin still hadn't had time for a sit-down with the guys. Her high from discovering one of their songs was on a movie soundtrack had worn off; now she was more than a little pissed they hadn't let her know what was coming. Caitlin had spoken to Bobby and he wasn't pleased either. They were going to have to establish some rules to keep everybody informed. No more surprises.

Martine didn't keep her long. She simply dropped her bomb and left. Caitlin had a minute to text Poppy Travis to see if she had time to comment on publicists and managers. She could have gone to any of her co-stars, but after getting to know Poppy while filming the band's first video, Caitlin thought talking to somebody who worked across various platforms would have some insider tips. Poppy did stage and screen; Caitlin did music and acting. She was going to need a publicist with a broad entertainment base. It was one more thing to add to her ever-growing list of things to do. They were all good things, but Caitlin was starting to feel like she was running out of energy keeping her plates in the air. Maybe having somebody to take a few of those plates, she could concentrate on the big picture instead of on the details. The more she thought about it, the more she liked the idea.

After that, it was back to work. With so many big names out sick, her character was filling a lot of blank spots in various scenes, even if it was as a placeholder. She was exhausted by the time production wrapped for the night. Sean was waiting in her trailer.

"Hey, you're here," she said, too tired to care she was stating the obvious. The tight lines around his eyes were a dead giveaway something was wrong. Caitlin placed her hands on the sides of his face and brushed her thumbs over his creased brow. "Did something happen?" she asked.

"Yes. We have to talk."

Her heart stuttered. Had she misjudged him? Run him off after one deep conversation? Guys weren't the only ones scared of those four words.

"I need to tell you what's going on with the vandalism at my house and some other things. Can we talk at your place?" he asked.

The band around her heart shifted and became a block of ice in her stomach. "Of course."

"Marcus is going to be there too," he added.

"Why?"

"Can we discuss this when we get there?" Sean asked.

"Absolutely." We need to talk. She hadn't known where she and Sean were headed. Apparently the trip was already over.

Chapter 13

THIS conversation was going to suck on many levels. The least of which was he had to apologize for dismissing Caitlin's worries about Shannon and Megan out of hand. Then he had to tell her she hadn't been concerned enough. He rubbed his breastbone when he was stopped at a red light. He glanced in the side view mirror to make sure Caitlin was with him. He wouldn't blame her if she peeled off and tried to lose him. Not that she could. Pacific Personal Security had a man on her who had started trailing her as soon as she cleared the studio gates. Sean hadn't told her about that yet. He wasn't taking any chance when it came to his safety. Or hers.

The police were getting nowhere with their case. Detective Brownlee kept him up-to-date, letting him know he'd spoken to both women. Shannon had reportedly burst into tears at the vandalism accusation. Megan made noises about filing harassment charges against him. Of the two, Sean was more worried about Shannon. She seemed less stable.

Megan was an unshakable bitch. He was used to dealing with bitches. His biggest concern was the utility corridor incident. He'd skipped that event when he'd filed his report. Getting caught off-guard was embarrassing. Kissing Megan didn't come close to what it was like to kiss Caitlin. There was no way he should have mistaken them, and he didn't want his heinous lack of judgment on record.

Caitlin didn't let him help her out of her car, or hold the door. She didn't let him in to her apartment past the galley kitchen. "Just say what you have to say and leave," she ordered.

"I'm sorry?" Sean knew he had a lot to apologize for, but he didn't know what, in particular, had pissed her off at the moment.

"Is that a question?"

"I know I need to apologize. I'm trying to figure out which part of what I'm about to say has pissed you off already."

She glared at him. "I don't want to put you out so I'll tell you. I don't appreciate you telling me you're fine with me putting my career first and then sleeping with me one more time before you dump me. If you had a problem with—"

Wait a minute. "Telling you what? Shit, Caitlin, I'm trying to tell you I'm in love with you and I'm going to do what it takes to protect you!"

Dead silence was not the reaction he was hoping for. Although it could have been worse. "You're in love with me?" she asked quietly.

"You think I'm trying to dump you?" His repeated question was much louder than hers. Before she had a chance to say anything even stupider, he backed her into her living room and pulled her into his lap on the sofa. "What the hell, Caitlin? I'm not breaking up with you. And, for the record, I'm not letting you break up with me either. Where is this coming from?" Had his stalker gotten to her and scared her off?

"Habit?"

Her voice sounded small. It was entirely wrong for any of the thousand and one personalities she'd displayed since he'd met her. Although this wasn't the conversation he wanted to have, it sounded like the one he needed to have with her. "Habit because?" he pressed.

"Because last night I told you my plans for global domination and that I was going to capitalize on Kara's death and you didn't blink. Guys always blink. I'm supposed to want to be successful—but not more successful than them. I figured 'We have to talk' was code for 'goodbye'. Since it's not, what did you want to talk about?"

Mistress of Misdirection she was not. Thank God. "No, let's stick with this conversation for a bit. I have no problem with you being more successful than me if it happens. No problem whatsoever." Sean was serious. He didn't have the drive or the desire to rule the world, which wasn't to say he didn't have a good work ethic. He knew what he wanted, which didn't include a house in the 'burbs with two-point-five kids, a dog, and a station wagon. Well, he wanted the dog. He was willing to work hard to play hard. He'd mostly been surprised Caitlin was up-front about her goals. That's when realization struck. "You've been dumped before because you work too hard, haven't you?"

"More than once," she confirmed.

"I'm not dumping you. For any reason. Especially not for something as stupid as that. If you achieve global domination, I will be cheering you on. Are we clear?" This was too important to fuck around with.

"Clear. And good, because breaking up with you would really suck," Caitlin added.

Sean felt the tension ease from her body. She shook her hair away from her face a few times. He assumed it was to ease the embarrassed flush he spotted under her tan. He was never one to ignore an opportunity to tease, but Caitlin's obvious distress held him back. Once she was again relaxed in his arms and her breath stopped hitching, she snuggled into his chest.

"I don't suppose you want to have make-up sex after our not-really-a-break-up fight?" Caitlin suggested.

He wanted. Unfortunately he still had to have his original security conversation with her, although he was less nervous about it now. Nothing was more serious than losing Caitlin. "We have to talk."

"Okay. Should things change, remember I offered to have sex with you now. If I get mad after this talk and change my mind, that's on you," she said.

"Fair enough," Sean agreed.

He told her everything. Almost everything. She'd been present at the confrontation at the Giving Back Foundation dinner. Sean didn't feel Caitlin needed to know about his second encounter with his ex-girlfriend. He'd make sure Megan never had another chance at him. He did admit Shannon had been outside the restaurant the night of their date. Caitlin growled a little at the news.

She growled a lot when he told her both Shannon and Megan had been at her premiere. "I can't believe I didn't spot them. I'm getting sloppy," she said.

"You had a lot on your mind. If Clancy hadn't grabbed you, I'm sure you would have noticed. Don't beat yourself up."

"I can't afford lapses in attention like that. It's dangerous."

This was a good an opening as he was going to get. "Unfortunately, it can be. Which is why I called Russ and Leo Vukovich. Leo assigned a bodyguard to you when you aren't on set or at home until the police finish investigating Megan and Shannon." He waited for her to explode. Then waited some more.

"Is this a knee-jerk he-man reaction or has an

assessment shown I actually need a bodyguard?" she asked carefully.

That was both an insulting and well-thought-out question. He understood the insulting part; Caitlin was used to taking care of herself. She'd told him growing up with her dad in the army meant she'd been smothered by enough overprotective men for one lifetime. But where had she learned about security assessments? "LAPD and Pacific Personal Security both say the vandalism at my house pushed it into the 'necessary' zone until they identify who it was."

"But you're thinking it's Megan or Shannon?"

Sean nodded. "Most likely. They're looking into other possibilities, just in case."

"A bodyguard, huh? I guess you should introduce me to my new best friend so I don't introduce him to my bear spray," Caitlin said.

"You're not going to argue?" He didn't want a fight, but this was too easy. How could he trust her if she were going to agree to his face and try to ditch her bodyguard as soon as he let his guard down?

"Sean, you do know what my dad does for a living?" she asked.

"He's in the army. An M.P., you said."

"That's right. Military police. Base security. Before I was a teenager, I learned more about home protection and self-defense through osmosis than most people learn in their entire lives. Later, I learned more on purpose. If trained people think this is necessary, I'll live with it. I'm not happy about it though."

"I think it's going to be Marcus. Are you all right with that?" he asked.

"I'll be fine. Will you be okay?"

"He's a professional. I'll be professional," Sean said.

Marcus wouldn't have a chance to do anything to or with Caitlin since Sean intended to be on the scene most of the time. Hopefully the other man wouldn't be around long. If Caitlin wasn't fazed by the situation, Sean was more than willing to let it drop for the moment and move on to more pleasant subjects.

"We are a pair of fucked-up individuals. Me and my career-killing presence, you and your stalker," Caitlin said. "But we seem to balance each other out pretty well. I'm glad I decided to keep you around."

"Me too." Sean couldn't believe she thought he was going to dump her. She had no idea of how deeply he was into her. How could she? He'd been falling for her for over a year. He'd been on her radar for less than a month. He wasn't going to deal with the fact that she hadn't said "I love you" back tonight. He'd pushed her far enough. He could wait for it. Not long, but he could wait.

* * * *

She was never going to get to sleep at this rate. Once she got her emotions under control from their non-break-up, Caitlin started analyzing the rest of their conversation. How could he say he loved her? They'd been on a handful of dates, and none of those had gone particularly well. Sean hadn't known her long enough to be in love with her. Lust, absolutely. Like, probably. She was still on her best-date behavior around him. Sean hadn't been with her through a severe PMS craving, or held her hand after a post-holiday phone call with her father when he asked when she was going to get a real job with some security and abandon her ridiculous dreams.

But he had seen her stumble and hadn't disappeared into the night. He surprised her by willingly playing second fiddle when she had to be in the spotlight. She'd never had a date do that without comment before. It gave credence to his comments about supporting her career. It was easier when she could look at him and see a man-whore. Now she had to give this new and improved Sean serious consideration.

Sean's cell phone bleated on the nightstand. Caitlin looked at her clock. 2:55 a.m. There was no way the call was good news. She turned on the bedside lamp as Sean sat up, then listened shamelessly to his half of the conversation.

"Hello? Speaking. What? Did you catch them? Any damage? Do I need to come down there? Okay. Yeah, fine, I'll file a report in the morning. Thanks."

He didn't put the phone away after he ended the call. "Do you have to go?" she asked.

"No." He didn't lie back down. He was still for a minute before he threw back the duvet. He stalked to her bedroom window, lifted the blind, and undid and reset the latch. "I'll be back in a minute."

Caitlin heard the blinds in the living room rustle. The deadbolt in her front door snapped open and shut. Sean was doing the house-check walk. She had a flashback of her dad doing the same thing when she was little whenever there was a news story about a home invasion. "Is everything locked to your satisfaction?" she asked when he returned to bed.

"Yep."

With the amount of tension radiating off him, Sean wasn't going to fall asleep anytime soon. Caitlin sidled up to him and burrowed under one shoulder so her head was on his chest. She petted his chest; not trying to do anything more than let him know she was there. When the arm around her finally relaxed, she rolled away to turn out the light. At least, she tried to.

Sean's arm tightened and pulled her back. "As an

FYI, I have a 9mm in my nightstand drawer. My dad started me with a girly, little .22. I upgraded because I have big hands. I also have a canister of bear spray on the shelf above my key hooks at the front door," Caitlin said quietly in the dimly lit room. "Various army officers who were friends of the family taught me self-defense all the way through high school. And I'm going to let Marcus be my shadow because I know how serious this is."

Sean grunted. "Somebody jumped the fence at my place tonight. Leo chased them off, but didn't catch them."

"Is your garage repaired and repainted?"

"It will be tomorrow. I don't know if it's safer for you here or at my house," he said.

"We'll take it as it comes."

They lay in silence for another minute before she noticed his hand had moved from her shoulder to her breast. Caitlin slid her hand down his stomach to where his chest hair turned coarser. He grabbed her fingers and halted her progress. "Not tonight," Sean said. He rolled them both over, pinning her on her back. "Tonight I want to touch you."

If he needed to inspect every square inch of her to make certain she was safe, she was fine with that. "Sean, I'm okay."

"I'm not. Give me this."

She couldn't offer another token protest. His mouth crashed down and silenced her. He bit her lip hard enough to make her squeak before she opened her mouth. Sean devoured her until she was breathless, and didn't stop. She gasped when he shifted his attention to her neck. "Sean? Honey, what's wrong?" Part of her understood he was reacting to the violation at his house. This was above and beyond what she expected.

"Nobody is getting to you." His voice was rough, pained. "I promise this shit isn't going to touch you. I'll take care of you." He stopped speaking and continued to make promises with his body. His tongue, his lips. He grabbed her hands and shoved them to the top of the mattress. "Hold on," he said. He shifted lower and concentrated on the breasts he'd been playing with while he kissed her.

Caitlin squirmed, unsure whether she was trying to get closer or farther from the tingling sensations spreading across her chest. Sean's thigh pinned her hips to the sheet. She'd never been with a man she trusted to hold her down while he had his naughty way with her. She bucked under him to see what he'd do.

He answered her silent question with a pinch on her nipple. Caitlin pressed her lips together to suppress a sub-vocal whine. He did it again. She couldn't hold back a second time. "Sean, I need..." She needed something.

"Didn't I say I'd take care of you?" Yes, he'd made that promise to her. She was so happy he was following through. Sean trailed his fingers across her flushed skin, over her stomach, then directly into the heat between her legs.

She was wet from his kisses and other attentions. The furious friction he gave her now had her arching herself into his hand. "Sean, please!" He swiped his tongue across her throbbing nipple and Caitlin shook from head to toe. When her tremors faded, she opened her eyes to see Sean staring down at her, the tension in his face finally gone. "That was wow." She tried to put some enthusiasm into her comment to show her appreciation of her world-class orgasm. Her final word came out in a croak.

"Glad to hear it." Sean flopped onto the mattress and

pulled her back to his side.

"Give me a minute and I'll return the favor," she offered.

"You already did me the favor. Now hush and go to sleep."

"But you didn't have a turn." Caitlin felt his rock-hard length pressing along the side of her thigh. She would have no problem falling back to sleep after coming so hard the back of her head almost blew off. She hesitated; she didn't want to leave Sean hurting.

"I got what I wanted. The sun's coming up in a couple hours. Close your eyes."

He stopped her hand from sliding past his waist. He curled his fingers around hers and pressed her palm into his chest over his heart. Caitlin stayed away long enough to hear Sean's breathing even out before she relaxed into her pillow. She didn't understand why he'd wanted to have such a one-sided encounter, but he was insistent…and she was really too sated to fight.

Chapter 14

IT had been an interesting, exhausting week and a half. Finally, the latest episode was wrapped and Sean was going to luxuriate in two days off in a row. Nothing but him, Caitlin, a full propane tank for grilling, and no social media whatsoever. He needed a break from online evisceration.

Sean was kicking himself for his habit of over sharing. He thought he'd been smart about it by only posting on his way out of a restaurant or bar. Apparently, that had been enough for people to be able to predict his schedule to an extent. Now they were staking out his favorite haunts. He'd had to find a new coffee shop since the location of his old one had been spread far and wide. Fortunately, Chris had recommended a small place that had opened a second location; Bella Bean made a killer cappuccino.

Shannon Tolliver had posted a heart-wrenching Internet plea for him to understand she was a true fan who would never hurt him and only wanted to show her loyalty to Eros. Not to him—to Eros—which made the whole thing more disturbing. The police had obviously scared her enough to keep her from making direct contact with him. Unfortunately it had done nothing to curb her digital stalking. She was leading the crusade of fans demanding he start posting his daily stops like he used to.

Megan, on the other hand, was directing a direct personal attack. He'd forgotten he'd given her his number at some point. He remembered now. Sean knew the exact moment the police visited her; his phone blew up. It took him five hours, sixty-one texts, and eighteen voicemails to get a new phone number.

The pair of women provided the information for a scathing entry in a gossip blog about Sean turning on his fans. They'd reported he'd sent the police after the two of them without mentioning the repeated vandalism attacks he'd suffered. Sean didn't know if the anonymous website didn't know or didn't care about his motivation. Fortunately, Layla came to his rescue.

She needed a hand at a quick appearance publicizing her drama camp for underprivileged children. It was hard to say Sean was ditching his fans when the next entry was about him making a charity appearance for kids.

It's not like he had anything else to do. It was a good thing most of his scenes had been with Caitlin, otherwise he never would have had a chance to see her. In the last eight days, they'd spent two nights together. She'd had two band rehearsals and was on her way to a third. Once it was done, she was all his. He planned to surprise her with a late, homemade supper.

"Hello?" he said into the phone's speaker.

"Hi. It's me. Rehearsal's been cut short. Bobby's sick as a dog. Do you want some company earlier than expected?"

Sean didn't try to fight his smile; though his blinding grin might have scared the couple in the station wagon beside him. "Absolutely. I'm not home yet. Do you want me to grab supper for you?"

"An apple cheddar salad from that place in the strip mall?" Caitlin requested.

He could do that. The deli had excellent roast turkey sandwiches as well. He could spend less time cooking and cleaning and more time burning off supper. "See you soon."

He hoped the call disconnected before Caitlin heard the crash. Sean jerked hard against his seatbelt before he slammed back into the low-riding seat. He got a glimpse in his rear view mirror before the massive grill behind him rammed his bumper and trunk again. He heard the dusty, white pick-up behind him rev for another run.

He looked out his window and saw he couldn't move left. A station wagon in the next lane was keeping pace with him, although the woman in the passenger seat was filming the encounter with a horrified look on her face. Sean checked the other side. He might have a sliver-thin window of opportunity.

The downside of driving a Maserati was it was going to lose in a collision against anything larger than a scooter. The upside was it was fast enough to avoid a collision if the person knew it was coming. Sean hit the gas and yanked the steering wheel right, jumping lanes before the pick-up driver had a chance to react. He cut across one more lane, gunned it into the emergency lane, to the rapidly approaching exit, and veered off at the last second.

Sean nearly ran a red light as he kept an eye peeled on his rear view mirror in case the truck somehow made it off the ramp. His rear bumper scraped the pavement and he could hear something rubbing a tire. He had to get off the road before it went flat.

A private garage sign a few blocks away caught his eye. Sean pulled his limping sports car along the side of the building out of view from the street. It took him two attempts to engage the parking brake. He dropped his trembling hands to his lap and began to swear, long and loud, pulling out curses he hadn't used since his UW locker-room days. When he'd burned off enough adrenaline to hold his hands steady, he pulled out his phone and brought up the number of the detective in charge of his case.

After a protracted conversation, Sean ended the call by agreeing to wait for the tow truck to take his car to the police impound lot to be forensically examined. Unfortunately, that left him stranded in the middle of nowhere.

"Hey, babe, there was an incident with the car. I've got a ride home, but I won't be able to stop for your salad." Sean was impressed at his casual tone. He wasn't going to freak Caitlin out by telling her what really happened when she was behind the wheel. If he could think of a way, he wouldn't tell her once she was safely inside his house, either. But he already knew that wasn't going to happen.

"No problem. Are you okay?"

"Fine," he lied. "Can you do me a favor? If you're getting your salad, do you want to grab me a roast turkey sandwich? And a side salad?" If he was going to drink like he wanted to when he got home, he'd need something in his stomach.

"Ranch for the salad and ketchup no mustard on the sandwich?" Caitlin asked.

He loved that she knew his order. "You got it."

"See you when you get to your place."

Hearing Caitlin's voice helped for a minute. As soon as he hung up, the tremors threatened to come back. Sean's next call was to Nick Thurston. He intended to ask for the number of the car service his friend used. Nick refused to give it to him. "Forget it. I'll come pick you up. Where are you?" the actor asked.

Sean had time for a cola from the garage's vending machine and tried to look as un-famous as he could while he waited for his ride. He breathed a sigh of relief when Nick appeared in a baseball cap driving Ashleigh's new, mid-range car.

"That's going to be an expensive fix," Nick said as he examined the hunk of destroyed fiberglass that used to be Sean's trunk. "Didn't you just get your car back from the body shop?"

Sean laughed. "I did. It looks great, doesn't it?"

"I can't see a single flaw on the door panels. What the hell happened to the rest of it?"

Sean had tried to keep the news of his stalker under wraps. All his work for nothing now. He thought he had it under control. He'd been wrong. Very wrong. He was going to need as many eyes as possible on Caitlin to keep her safe, so he filled his friend in on the events of the past two weeks. "I was on my way home when somebody rammed me from behind. Repeatedly. I don't know if they wanted me to crash or to run me off the road or what. I'm just thankful Caitlin wasn't in the car with me," Sean said.

"Shit. You called the cops, right? Have you called Leo Vukovich to let him know your stalker has upped the ante?"

"I'll do it when I get home." Sean had cancelled the bodyguards after Shannon and Megan attacked him through the media, but stayed away from him directly. The police couldn't do much about online comments. As long as the women kept their distance, Sean didn't care. Now he regretted giving them the benefit of the doubt. "Caitlin's going to be staying with me until this is taken care of."

Nick got them back onto the freeway and headed toward Sean's house. "Speaking of Leo, I've been in contact with him and Russ. They sent me a copy of the quotes they're going to give Ashleigh for her studio and apartments. The one I want her to get for the building is going to be too expensive for her. She's doing well in her new location, but not well enough to afford the top of the line system. Realistically, it is overkill for the neighborhood, except Ash and Caitlin have made names for themselves. They're attracting more attention than normal. I'm going to ask Leo if he can quietly drop a couple thousand off the installation estimate and have him bill me for the difference," Nick said. He could easily afford the minor subterfuge. Nick's girlfriend, Ashleigh Jessup, like Caitlin, was fiercely independent. It was probably one of the reasons why they were friends. Unlike Cait, Ashleigh ran her own business, a dance studio. She wouldn't appreciate Nick's intervention. In this case, discretion was the better part of valor.

"Would the system you prefer work for Caitlin's suite too?" Sean asked.

Nick knew what his real question was. "Yes. Do you want me to have Leo's billing department contact you?"

"I'll do it." Caitlin had been surprisingly understanding about the bodyguard. She didn't need to know about the security system. If anything, Nick would have to explain himself to Ashleigh about going behind her back and upgrading her security system, but only if Leo violated his confidentiality clause. Sean suspected Ashleigh wouldn't put up much of a fight if and when she eventually found out.

"What are you going to tell Caitlin about the car?" Nick asked.

"I'll have to tell her the truth since it means she's getting her bodyguard back. If this fucker scares her off, I'm going to kill 'em when I find 'em." Yes, the cops had two female suspects. Sean didn't have their experience, but this level of violence felt male to him. It didn't matter; he'd be ready for whoever came at him.

"How serious are you about Caitlin?" Nick sounded surprised. He'd played Sean's wingman in the field for the last couple years and was used to Sean's rotating selection of arm candy.

"I'm serious."

"Serious serious? Because you know you might have to work with her for a while."

"I'm inviting her to Easter dinner in April with my family," Sean said. Caitlin didn't know it yet, though. He expected some skepticism with his history, but he was only going to tolerate it once. "You know, you and Ash weren't the most conventional couple either. In fact, you had even less in common. I'm not going to screw this up, Nick."

His friend took his eyes from the road to give him a hard look. "Good. You both deserve to be happy. Keep in mind your friends and Caitlin's friends have all kinds of connections with each other. If this goes bad, it might not just be you."

"It's not going to go bad. I'll make it work." And the first part of making it work was taking care of his stalker.

* * * *

Caitlin was exhausted. Being an adult was hard work. She needed two days off in the worst way, and not two days off from filming so she could spend the entire time rehearsing with the band and working on new material. She needed two days in a cave with a blanket and a cooler full of sandwiches and bottled waters. But she couldn't bitch about it. Oh, poor me, being on a hit show and having an album burning up the charts and being offered a movie deal. It's terribly stressful. Show me sympathy. Yeah, that wasn't going to happen. She'd have been more appreciative and less grumpy if it all hadn't hit in the same sleepless week.

She was so busy being a professional, she was neglecting her personal life. Sean was great about it. He said he understood things were nuts right now. Still, a part of her waited for him to throw in the towel.

Olympus was rolling along. Chris would be back on Monday in time to start filming the next episode. Jessica returned a few days after her accident and was limping along. Thankfully, Caitlin's own character Psyche wasn't going to be a major player for the next couple episodes, giving her more downtime. She couldn't believe they were halfway through the season already.

Her agent was working on the movie contract. The small part in the low-budget psychological would make a great stepping stone to other, bigger roles. Caitlin knew roughly when she'd be available for filming; now she was waiting to hear if she could make it work with Charlie Oscar Echo. They were going to be a problem.

Caitlin had dreamed of the day when the band would hit the big time. Deep down, she never truly expected it would arrive. Now it was here. The soundtrack to Three Date Rule debuted in the Top 100 the week the movie opened. It cracked the Top 50 during the second week of release. The band's own album hadn't moved over to the big lists, but Watching Him Watching Her had hit the top ten singles on the indie charts.

"I'm fine," Bobby Wheaton insisted for the third time, as he brushed a sweat-damp lock of blond hair from his forehead. "It's the fucking sushi Greg made me try. I knew raw fish was a bad idea. Let's get this rehearsal over with. I never thought I'd be saying this. Which clubs do we want to play and which ones are we giving a pass?"

Caitlin couldn't believe it either. After years of scrambling to find a couple venues a month, these days they had clubs who'd turned them down for years calling them for gigs. They couldn't play them all if they wanted to.

Peter Blackwood and Greg Mills kept glancing at her as they discussed the pros and cons of each date and venue. Caitlin tried as hard as she could to ignore their looks, but she couldn't avoid the elephant in the room anymore. Somebody had to break first, and it was going to be her.

Charlie Oscar Echo was a garage band when they were kids. They were grown up now and looking at careers. This soundtrack was their big break. They had to strike while the iron was hot. If they didn't do everything possible to capitalize on their current momentum, they might as well quit now. That meant more local shows, touring, and putting out another album as soon as possible. She could swing it—probably—if she concentrated on the band during the show's hiatus. If she took the movie role, there was no way she could give her music, and the guys, the time and attention they deserved. Caitlin had to make her decision before she ruined their chances.

"Before we decide on the new dates, I have an announcement," she said.

The room went silent, almost as if the others knew what she was going to say.

"There's a strong possibility I'm going to be offered a big role in an upcoming picture."

"Cait-girl, that's fantastic! Congratulations," Bobby said, smiling. He stood and raised his arms to hug her, then changed directions and bolted for the bathroom.

Peter was more subdued. "Congratulations," he said

quietly. He was always quiet when he was thinking. "When will you be filming?"

"Right in the middle of your proposed tour dates," she admitted. Either the band had to sacrifice two months of prime concert dates in September and October, or they needed a replacement bassist. Either way, Caitlin was out. They knew it.

"Do you want to deal with this right now?" Greg asked.

"Can we let it go until I have the signed contract in hand?" she countered.

"Absolutely. It won't mean you're off the hook for song writing," he said.

"Or recording new songs featuring the exquisite Ms. Kelly," Peter ordered.

"Or dropping by our shows on occasion," Greg added.

"You're basically saying you own my soul and I'll never get away from you," Caitlin said. She smiled brightly despite the fact her eyes burned with unshed tears.

"Never," they promised.

Her boys were the best. They were letting her off easy, especially when they could have made it both painful and costly for her to leave the band. They were also asking her to keep a foot in the door, which was exactly what she'd hoped for. She hadn't been sure she'd get it. She even had some time to enjoy the ride to the top. "I love you all." She aimed for sarcastic, but her voice cracked.

"I love you all too, except for Greg. He's a bastard," Bobby shouted from the bathroom.

"And there goes the mood. Thanks, Bobby, we can always count on you," Greg said.

"Fuck off, you poisoning shit. I'm dying in here. What did you give me?"

"A Dynamite roll. It had deep fried shrimp in it. Nothing raw. Quit bitching about the sushi. It was probably one of those burritos you get from those stupid street trucks," Greg yelled back.

The closed door did nothing to muffle the sound of Bobby vomiting up a lung. Caitlin lost any desire for dinner. "Are we calling this a night?" she asked.

Her call to Sean to tell him rehearsal was cancelled netted her dinner, although his later call cancelled it. Even if she had to buy her own meal, she was happy to be heading to his house. She wanted a quiet place to hide until she had to deal with everything on Monday. If this was the end of life as she knew it, she was glad she was spending it with Sean.

Chapter 15

"**THIS** is not an incident. An incident implies you still have the vehicle. What happened?" Caitlin asked. She was waiting on the front step when Ashleigh's car pulled into his driveway. It wasn't a nag; it was more like a what-the-hell-are-you-okay.

Nick didn't open the door, or roll down his window. As soon as Sean stepped out, he waved and slammed the car into reverse. Apparently Nick knew more about how Caitlin was going to respond to this conversation than he'd let on.

"I'm fine. My car, not so much," Sean told her. "Let's talk about it inside." He felt too exposed outside, especially considering how easily an intruder had twice pierced his security.

"I don't want to talk about it insi—Fuck, really?" Caitlin spun on her heel and stomped through the open door into his living room, where she pulled the curtains closed and threw herself on his couch. "Really? They did something to your car? What? Did one of those whackos cut your brake line or something? Why aren't the police here taking your statement? Why aren't there any security people here? Did you call them and tell them you needed your bodyguard back?"

"Cait, breathe." The more she panicked and the louder she got, the more relaxed and happier he felt. Caitlin wasn't much for declaring her feelings, he'd found, not when she wasn't on stage. For such a passionate person, she kept a tight hold on her emotions.

She still hadn't told him she loved him. Not in those exact words. The words she was using now, however, were pretty much the same thing.

"Nobody cut my brake line or tampered with my car. Somebody rammed me on the freeway. I've already spoken to Detective Brownlee. I gave him my initial statement over the phone and I'm seeing him tomorrow. They're picking up my car to go over it for evidence. The bodyguards are on their way. I'm fine, Cait," he said in his most level tone. His glow at having Caitlin worry about him quickly evaporated when he saw she was still shaking after his explanation.

"They rammed you? How's your neck? How's your back? Do you have a masseuse on speed dial? Or a chiropractor?" Her voice got louder at the end of every question, but she wrenched it back down to normal levels each time.

Sean settled in the corner of the couch. Then he stretched, grabbed Caitlin, and pulled. She lost her balance and fell against his chest. She struggled against him as she tried to sit up. He refused to relax the grip he had on her. He didn't try to reason with her. She had all the information he had. Instead, he pressed her cheek to his chest and stroked his fingers through her long hair. "I'm fine. I promise," he repeated, his lips brushing her ear.

It took ages for the tension to leave her body. "I think I'm going to put you on a leash," she eventually said.

"Sounds kinky."

"Don't get excited. I'm giving it to your bodyguard to hold. If you get more than four feet from him, it's going to shock you. Sean, I know you're trying to downplay things, but this isn't an over-exuberant fan or regular pissed-off ex-girlfriend. They aren't just following you. They're actively trying to kill you. You have to protect yourself."

He wouldn't say kill him. Shake him up, make him pay attention, sure. Would they have stopped before they killed him? *Nobody hates me enough to want me dead, right?* Caitlin climbed off him to bring their food into the living room. Sean didn't move. *Right? They were trying to scare him.*

He texted Russ again while Caitlin was in the kitchen. He felt a little more comfortable with Russ than Leo, although the two men were brothers. Russ had been a friend for years before going into the security business; the man had locked Sean out of his trailer in his tighty whities. Sean could ask him some potentially embarrassing questions without worrying about looking stupid.

Almost there, Russ texted back.

Sean made it through supper with a smile on his face, even though the Panini bun stuck to the roof of his dry mouth. The more he thought about Caitlin's rant, the quieter he got. She'd ripped off the very comfortable blinders he'd been wearing. Ramming somebody on a freeway with a full-sized truck was not a declaration of misplaced love. They wanted to take him out of the picture permanently. When Russ finally arrived, Sean took him into his office while Caitlin said she was going to take a bath.

"The fucker in the truck was trying to kill me, wasn't he?" Sean said as soon as the door was closed.

"You're just figuring this out now? I thought that was why you called us," Russ said.

At 6'5", Sean looked down on almost everybody. Russ was six feet even, but he was a lot wider than Sean.

His bulk more than compensated for his lack of height. As a big black man in a dark suit designed to intimidate, Russ would make anyone coming at Sean think twice. Unless his attacker had a gun and could drop Russ before they got into arm's reach. Maybe Sean should request somebody who wasn't a good friend to watch his back. It would be safer for them. A bodyguard's job was to be in the line of fire. It would be easier on Sean if he didn't know the person risking his life for him. "Maybe you should be on Caitlin and Marcus should be on me," Sean said.

"I know what you're thinking. It doesn't work that way. I've known you longer, I know your habits. The same goes for Marcus and Caitlin. If we don't play to our strengths, we're not doing our jobs right."

If Russ insisted on standing by him, Sean couldn't stop him. He could do something about Caitlin though. "If Caitlin and I weren't going out, she'd be safer, wouldn't she?" he asked. An idea was forming. She wasn't going to like it.

"Maybe," Russ replied noncommittally.

"If she weren't in the picture, they'd stay away from her," Sean continued. This could work. If they pretended to break up, Megan or Shannon or whoever the fuck was driving the truck would have no reason to go after Caitlin. Sean ignored the fact they hadn't gone after her yet.

"You could try. I wouldn't recommend it."

"Why not?" The more he thought about it, the more Sean liked the idea.

"Two reasons. One, if you break up with her, she won't have any need for a bodyguard. That means either you put a guy on her and basically announce she means something to you, or you don't put a guy on her and leave her defenseless if your stalker decides to make sure she stays out of the picture," Russ said.

Sean could find another way to put a bodyguard on Caitlin. He'd manufacture an excuse if he had to. "What's the other reason?"

"If you want to stay away from Caitlin, you have to break-up with her, or pretend to do it. I don't think she's going to be willing to go for either option."

"She'll be fine once I explain it to her."

Russ's eyes got comically wide. "Dude, I know you aren't one for long term relationships, but have you ever seriously dated a woman? Logic is not compatible with love. If Caitlin has any feelings for you, she's not going to turn them off and leave you when she thinks you need her. If anything, she's going to stick closer than ever."

Sean didn't want to admit Russ was probably right. When Russ and Layla had first started dating, Russ was injured on the Olympus set after a stunt rehearsal. Layla temporarily overcame a crippling phobia of hospitals to make sure he was okay. Caitlin was strong and stubborn enough not to do anything less. Maybe if he explained and got Russ to back him up. Caitlin was smart. She'd get it.

"No. Absolutely not," she said.

Perhaps she didn't understand the plan.

*

"No fucking way in hell. Are you crazy?" was Caitlin's preferred response. Unfortunately, with Sean's current, protective attitude, he'd probably say she was thinking emotionally rather than rationally, and then she'd have to kill him. What kind of plan involved them fake-breaking up? That ploy had a one-hundred percent fail rate. It was historically documented. Evidently Sean had never read Romeo and Juliet in high school.

"Let me explain," Sean said. Russ had shown his intellect when he left the room after Sean asked her to join him on the leather sofa against the wall. It was just the two of them, and Sean had assured her during earlier escapades that the room was completely soundproof.

"No. It'll be too hard for me to kick your ass from a seated position. Sean, what is wrong with you?" she asked.

That was a rhetorical question. He was attempting a hero maneuver. He seemed to be missing the part where she wasn't the one who needed saving.

"Caitlin, I'm suggesting this for your own good," he said. Softly. Patiently.

If there was one phrase guaranteed to set her off, 'for your own good' was it. She'd suffered from it and by it until she was old enough to decide for herself what was good for her. "Let me tell you about 'for my own good.' Starting a new school every year and a half as my dad was transferred instead of letting me live with a host family so I could finish high school in the same town was 'for my own good' because it brought me to new places to have new experiences with new people. Today I have five high school friends I'm still in contact with. Five. And I work with three of them. Leaving me on my own overnight as soon as it was legal, when my dad was overseas and my mom had to work, was 'for my own good' because it taught me how to take care of myself. I don't remember a time when I was little when I could knock on their bedroom door and get a hug after having a bad dream."

Caitlin paused to take a breath. She knew she had to stop but she couldn't hold it back. Sean opened his mouth. She held up a finger. "For my own good was the reason I got no support when I said I wanted to be an actress, or when I moved to LA, or when I broke my engagement with Neil, who, according to my father, was a fine catch and it should be my honor to support. For my own good has screwed me my entire life, Sean. Don't you shove that shit down my throat and expect me to thank you."

She bit her tongue and tasted blood. She didn't let the pain show. Caitlin would fight Sean as long as she had to in order to make him see the light.

He was silent as he stared at her. "I'm guessing there are issues there," he said.

"One or two." Million.

"Will you at least listen to my plan?" he asked.

"Sure." Because listening didn't mean agreeing.

"Thank you. If we pretend to break up, you won't be at risk because this psycho won't know you matter to me. You'll be safe. That's important to me, Caitlin. Maybe the most important thing." Sean held her hand as he spoke, and pressed it against his chest. "Do you understand why we should do this?"

"I have some questions about the particulars. How long should we break up for? Because, unless you know an arrest is imminent, 'indefinitely' is not an option I'm willing to work with," she said.

"We could put a time limit on it," Sean suggested.

"If we were apart, we'd have to date other people to maintain the charade. We'd have to go out with them and kiss them in public to make it look real, right?" she asked.

Sean frowned at her. "I don't think dating other people is necessary. We wouldn't have to jump right into new relationships to get the media time to sell the break-up. It wouldn't be for that long," he protested.

"If we break up and get back together after however

long, if the cops don't catch your stalker, the only thing different between our situation now and our situation then is that we'll have wasted months we could have been together," she argued. "It's not going to help anybody. We haven't even addressed the fact that I've never been targeted. It's very sweet and heroic, but it's a horrible idea, Sean."

He kissed her fingertips and set her hand back in her lap. The vein in his forehead throbbed a frantic beat, but he didn't say a word. This was a make or break argument. Sean had said his piece. She'd said hers. Now it was his turn again. Caitlin hoped he realized if he pressed her, she'd agree to break up with him. However, he had to understand it would be a permanent move on her part. She never hid who she was, and she wasn't about to start now. Not even for him.

"I really, really hate this," he finally said.

"Me too."

"I don't know what to do," he admitted.

"How about we catch this bitch so we can stop worrying about it?"

"That works for me. You're still getting a bodyguard. That's not an option."

"That's fine." She could live with that. It was a smart decision. His vein stopped pounding as soon as she agreed.

"And a GPS tracker in a lipstick tube in your purse like in the spy movies," Sean added.

"Temporarily," she said.

"And I'm getting you a collar and a leash too. But only for the bedroom," he continued.

"Nice try." Her giggles cut the tension. She'd won the battle. If the situation dragged on for long, Caitlin knew the conversation would repeat itself. She needed

Russ and Leo and the cops to end this soon, one way or another, or the next time wouldn't have this kind of happy ending.

Chapter 16

SEAN wasn't going to lie. It was weird waking up with a stranger in his house—not Caitlin, she was welcome—but Russ rambling around in his kitchen precluded his ability to get coffee in his underwear. Sean was still willing to trade privacy for protection. He grabbed a pair of sweatpants and left Caitlin sleeping in his bed.

What a shitty night. Caitlin had been less than impressed with his fake break-up plan. He'd thought of it on the fly and Caitlin pointed out some significant flaws. Russ smirked when Sean told him they were abandoning that line of attack. He could live with some minor embarrassment.

The good part was only good for him. After dinner and a movie to unwind, he and Caitlin had fallen into bed. The sex was as good as always, but Caitlin's light humor didn't flow as easily as it usually did. Sean figured it was carry-over from their earlier fight. Until the crying started in the middle of the night.

At first he thought she was upset with him, especially when she didn't respond when he called her name. He turned his bedside lamp on and saw her eyes squeezed shut and a tear rolling down her cheek. That was when he realized she wasn't awake. She was caught in one of the bad dreams she'd told him about.

But unlike before, now Caitlin had somebody she could go to for a hug. Sean gently shook her awake. "Caitlin, Cait, wake up. It's not real. You're dreaming," he said quietly.

It was scary. She didn't make any noise after she opened her eyes. No crying, no gasping for air, nothing. She didn't look at him. "I dreamed you were gone. I'm fine."

She wasn't kidding when she'd said she trained herself not to need anybody. So he didn't wait for her to ask. He wrapped his arms around her and pulled her to his chest. "It's just a dream," he said again.

Sean watched the clock over the top of her head. It took the better part of an hour for Caitlin to fall asleep again. She didn't say a word for the whole time. He held her; she let him. When she did finally nod off and the tension drained from her body, Sean felt like he'd finished first in a marathon.

He woke up feeling pretty good until he saw what was playing on the television after pouring his first cup of coffee for the morning. "Where did they get that?" he asked Russ before he answered his own question. "The couple in the station wagon."

The shaky video showed him talking to somebody, evidently over a speaker since the car was empty. His Maserati jerked wildly before he straightened it out. It swerved again after the second impact and Sean watched himself try to bring the car back into the lane again before he yanked on the wheel and disappeared out of frame. The video shooter caught one more glimpse of him as he tore down the off-ramp before the truck that hit him sped away. "At least the cops have a better description of the truck now," Sean joked.

Russ didn't laugh. "Wait 'til you hear who was driving it," he said.

Sean waited for the entertainment reporter to continue her report. "It's unconfirmed. Some sources say

Sean Glenn's co-star and girlfriend Caitlin Kelly was driving the pick-up and went after him in a jealous rage. Perhaps Sean's widely reported playboy past has resurfaced. I'm sorry to say it, folks. Olympus's favorite couple may be on the rocks."

"Did I hear right? They're saying Caitlin tried to kill me because I cheated on her?" Those miserable motherfuckers! His "widely reported playboy past" had faded into history months ago. Not to mention, casting Caitlin as the bad guy? That was insane.

He realized he'd set his coffee mug down on the counter harder than he intended when the handle snapped off in his hand. That was also when he noticed he was grinding his teeth to the point he could feel the vibrations in his ears.

"How about you take it down a notch?" Caitlin whispered in his ear. She wrapped her arms around him and gave him a squeeze as she quickly pecked his cheek. "Hi, Russ," she said to the kitchen's other occupant.

"You aren't upset at this?" Russ asked, gesturing at the television.

"I know we're not on the rocks. I'm more frustrated because you know Martine is going to call us on our weekend off about this." Caitlin grabbed Sean's damaged cup, dumped what was left down the sink, and tossed the mug into the trash.

The blinding rage that had been building dropped to more manageable levels the second Caitlin had touched him. He was still pissed off, but hearing her say she trusted him without a hint of hesitation reminded him the reporter's bullshit was outside his house, not inside it.

She handed him a fresh cup of coffee, with milk. It was a little lighter than he liked it, but he sipped it with a smile since Caitlin had memorized how he liked to take his morning pick-me-up.

"Don't do anything stupid. I already lost the band. I don't want to lose you too. I don't do visiting days at prisons. Pat-downs are not sexy," she added.

He saw he and Russ had matching raised eyebrows before the bodyguard excused himself. "What do you mean you lost the band? Did they kick you out?" Sean asked.

"I kinda kicked myself out. We all agreed it had to be done," she said. Tight lines radiated from the corner of her eyes, but her voice was steady as she relayed her news.

"Why?" He'd only seen her at one show. Even with his limited exposure he knew losing the band was a huge chunk of herself. He couldn't imagine a situation where she'd willingly walk away.

"Something had to give. They were talking about touring, and once I get this movie role, I'm booked through our hiatus. I can't ask them to stall their careers indefinitely, especially not with the attention Charlie is getting right now. I've decided to step back. They're going to start looking for a replacement bassist," she explained.

She didn't look overly upset. Her eyes shone a little bit, but her voice was steady. He got the impression that she was used to making hard decisions, although this one seemed particularly cruel. Sean bit back his comment that the reason the band was doing well was because of Caitlin's movie. It didn't seem fair she had to quit when things were starting to pick up. She'd put in the work; now some asshole was going to reap the benefits.

"It's okay. Charlie Oscar Echo is like the mafia. I'll never be totally out. Priorities, right?"

"Why didn't you tell me about this last night? You

must have been upset," Sean said. He knew she held herself back, but this was huge. She should have shared.

"Are you serious? You were trying to break up with me last night. Priorities. Yeah, I love the band, but I love you more. I had to deal with what was more important."

I love you more. Caitlin finally said the words and then she went back to her coffee like it was nothing. "What was that?" Sean asked.

"You were more important," she repeated.

He loved hearing that too, but, "No, the other part."

"I love you. Okay?" Her face turned red, and she took half a step back. Almost like she was afraid of his response to her declaration.

"Definitely okay. Wonderfully okay. We-should-go-upstairs-and-celebrate okay," he said. He took her mug and set it on the counter.

"I wasn't done with that."

"I'll bring you breakfast in bed once I'm done with you," Sean promised. He knew it was a lie. With the list of dirty things he wanted to do to her, it would more likely be lunch. Maybe supper.

* * * *

Sean was too good to be true. He was the best guy she'd ever dated. Caitlin was beginning to think he could be the one. The revelation scared her; she'd never come close to assigning a man that number. She never would have guessed Sean would have been the guy to hit all her buttons.

Ooh. Like that one. The man had radar to previously hidden erogenous zones. Caitlin shivered when he found another one. Sean blew on the pulse point at her elbow, and the cool air on her sweat-damp skin set her off again. "You are so much fun to play with," Sean said, smiling down on her.

"Why don't I show you how much fun I can be?" Caitlin asked. She groped under the sheet until she found what she was looking for.

"Um, Cait…"

If he could speak coherently, she was obviously doing something wrong. She wrapped her fingers around his hard length. "I'm sorry. I didn't mean to leave this here alone and neglected while you took care of me. I should remedy the situation immediately."

The heat of his shaft warmed her hand. She managed to stroke him a couple times before Sean rolled on top of her. "You can play another day. I need to be inside you now," he said.

She needed him too. It was a need. Caitlin had to show him what she felt for him since she'd held back on the words. She had to know he was still with her, that his words about breaking up were only pretend and he really didn't want her gone.

His look told the truth. Sean's eyes blazed with need and hunger. "Do I need to—"

"No. Hurry." She was wet enough.

Sean entered her hard and fast. The edge of pain at the sudden fullness forced her eyes closed for a moment. "God, Sean, yes!" She matched his movements, her hips rolling in concert with his.

"Do you have any idea how good this feels?" Sean asked, his breath punctuated by gasps.

Even though he kept most of his weight on his forearms, he was big enough that his chest pinned her to the mattress. Her shallow breaths grew more frantic as adrenalin and excitement flooded her bloodstream.

"Come for me, Cait. Now," he ordered.

Caitlin stopped fighting and let her instincts do as they willed. Her back arched as every cell in her body contracted at the same time, then relaxed with a groan. She felt Sean's tenseness thrumming through her. She wrapped her arms around his shoulders and hooked her fingers on the thick skin on his back. The bite of her nails drove him over the edge.

Sean kissed the hollow of her throat, then worked his way up her jaw to her mouth. He groaned too, and his smile said he did it deliberately. It worked. She laughed.

He dropped beside her. "Yeah, I'm never giving you up. You might kill me with fantastic sex, but..." His voice trailed away.

"But what? I just told you I loved you. You can say it."

"But losing you would definitely do the job. I love you, Caitlin. In case there is any question in the future, I'm in love with you. I promise not to suggest we break up again."

"If you do, I promise to fight with you until you change your mind." Caitlin had waited a long time for a man like him. For him.

Chapter 17

MONDAY morning came much too early. His insurance offered him a rental, but Sean left it at home. He liked carpooling with Caitlin since they were on the same schedule for the moment. He knew it was the new-love thing making him grasp at every a minute he could get with her.

It was also a not-so-subtle "in your face" to the media outlets who were reporting Caitlin had been driving the pick-up that rammed him. Chris and Nick—he assumed it was them—arranged bright orange pylons around their vehicles and formed a large protective barrier around Caitlin's spot. She didn't say a word when she saw it.

"What are you thinking?" he asked.

"I think I need a car jack and seven minutes when nobody's watching the parking lot," she said.

"Why?"

"Chris doesn't have a four-wheel drive. I need to raise the axle enough for the tires to brush the ground. We can sit here and watch him spin his wheels. Free entertainment."

"And I thought I was evil."

"Have you not been watching the news?" she teased. On Saturday morning, Sean had been concerned about the story swirling through various news reports. Even the truth could be battered and bruised if lies were thrown against it often enough. Caitlin disappeared upstairs for a while and Sean heard her on some kind of conference call with Sydney and Ashleigh. Curses and laughter floated down the hall, and when she came back downstairs an hour later, she was in a much better mood. She called a moratorium on the news by Saturday afternoon, and they hadn't heard it mentioned again until a radio announcer mentioned it on the way to work.

"You're joking about it now?" Sean asked.

"It is a joke. We were the last thing mentioned in that radio segment. It'll be out of the news cycle by the end of the day at this rate," Caitlin said. She bent to tie her shoe and snuck a peek at Chris's undercarriage while she was close to the ground. "Yeah, that'll work. No problem."

He didn't know how she managed to pull it off, but she did. When they pulled out of the lot at the end of the day, Chris was slamming his hand against his steering wheel. Caitlin tooted her horn and waved as they drove by, and Chris's frustrated face turned to one of shock and awe. "How long do you think it'll take for him to figure it out?" she asked.

"Now that he knows you did something? Not long," Sean said. He let her drive in silence a while longer. She'd been right; there hadn't been any chatter about her being the driver who'd hit him. Everybody had asked if he was okay. That was the extent of it. Unfortunately, he'd heard rumblings of something even worse. "Did you hear anything today?"

"About me totaling your Maserati? No."

Fuck. He didn't want to spoil her day. "You know the writers have been playing this season close to the vest, right?"

"Not really. This is my first year. I wouldn't know any differently. Why?" Caitlin asked.

"Rumor has it they are going to be killing someone off in the last episode."

She took her eyes off the road long enough to give him a good, hard look. "And you think it might be me?"

"You are one of three humans on the cast."

"They could kill off anybody. Even one of the guest stars. It doesn't mean it's me."

"I hope not," Sean agreed. His bad feeling didn't dissipate.

"Look. We have enough going on. Let's not borrow trouble, okay?"

He lifted her hand off the gearshift and kissed her knuckles. "Okay. Your place?"

"I miss my bed."

Sean needed to buy her a new bed. A California King so his feet weren't hanging over the edge of the mattress. Although, waking up curled around Caitlin did have its benefits.

His phone started blowing up at five in the morning, way too early for civilized people when there weren't award nominations involved. Caitlin beat him to it the first time and slapped the ignore button. She cuddled into him without ever opening her eyes. She did open them for the second call to glare at the screen. When his phone went off a third time, she handed it to him. "It sounds important."

He recognized the blurry name attached to the caller-ID. "Clark, do you know what time it is?"

His agent didn't waste time with niceties. "Where are you?"

"I'm in bed. Why?"

"Whose bed?"

"Excuse me?"

"Do you know a woman named Megan Unger?"

He patted Caitlin's arm as he prowled down the hall to her living room. "Yes. She's one of the people the police are investigating for the vandalism. You know that," Sean said.

"Did you fuck her?" his agent asked.

"Excuse the fuck you?"

"Did you have sex with the woman?"

"Yes. Months ago."

"She's claiming you got her pregnant. She's hired a lawyer who sent out a press release. They're filing a paternity suit. It's everywhere, Sean. We can't shut this down," Clark said.

He couldn't shut it down? Clark Greene was the one of the best in the game at damage control, not that Sean had put his skills to the full test. This should have been minor compared to some of the fires Clark had put out for his other clients. "Why not?" Sean carefully pulled back a section of curtain and peeked out the window that over looked the road in front of the building. Two cars were running, their exhaust visible in the pre-dawn light. "I think Caitlin's got paparazzi staking out her apartment."

"I wouldn't doubt it. This is ugly, Sean. We need to meet. Can you get out of there unseen?"

He could. It would involve Marcus, Russ, Leo, and a shell game before it got too light outside. Getting Caitlin out would be impossible. She was the wrong shape and size to pass for any of the guys. "I can. What about Caitlin?" Sean asked.

"She isn't my concern. You are," Clark said.

"She's my concern," Sean growled. He was not going to leave Caitlin swinging in the breeze while he covered his own ass. Her patience with him was going to run out pretty damned fast at this rate. Having a stalker was enough stress to break them up, but she'd hung in like a champ. A paternity suit, no matter how fictional, could very well be the last straw.

"She's got her own people to deal with situations like this. Get yourself to my office and we'll try to get this somewhat contained," Clark ordered.

Five minutes to call Leo Vukovich. Five minutes to shower. It would take another fifteen for Leo and Russ to arrive as a distraction, and half an hour to get to Clark's office…"I'll see you in an hour," Sean said before he ended the call. He wasted thirty seconds trying not to punch a hole in Caitlin's living room wall before he sucked it up and made his calls. He chickened out on waking Caitlin and ducked into her bathroom.

She was awake and sitting in the middle of the bed when he went into the bedroom to get his clothes after his shower. "You aren't the sneak out the morning after type. Who was on the phone?" she asked.

"Clark. My agent."

"And what did Clark, your agent, want at this hour?"

He was going to have to check to see if she'd taken any journalism classes at some point because her questions left him no wiggle room. "Megan is causing trouble again."

"Five o'clock in the morning trouble? That's not vandalism."

He captured both her hands in his. It would make it harder for her to run. "She's filing a paternity suit against me."

It hurt when Caitlin tried to pull away. She didn't struggle after her first jerk. It still broke off a piece of his heart, no matter how much he understood the reaction to his news. "It's bullshit, Cait. If she is pregnant, it isn't mine. I haven't been with her in months. Before the charity dinner, I hadn't seen her since last summer." He didn't raise his voice. It wasn't Caitlin he was mad at.

"A paternity suit? She can't drop a bomb like that

without something to back it up."

That's what worried him. He knew he was in the clear, but he knew it wasn't going to be as easy as he said/she said. "She doesn't have anything, Cait. Nothing. I didn't touch her. I swear." The band around his chest eased when he felt her fists relax. Sean worked his fingers between hers. "I've got to go to Clark's office to get a handle on this before it spins further out of control. Marcus, Russ and Leo are going to help me get out of your apartment unseen because there are already reporters outside. They'll be waiting for you. I'll have one of the guys escort you to the studio. If they do get to you, stick with 'No comment', okay?"

She nodded.

It killed him not to pull her close and demand her mouth for a good-bye kiss. Instead, he pulled her head down and kissed her forehead. "I'll call you as soon as I have any news but you should probably keep your phone off. I'll get a hold of whoever's with you to tell you to turn it on." He left her, alone in her bed, hurting, to deal with his problem.

Megan Unger was going to pay.

* * * *

Caitlin nodded at Leo Vukovich, lifted her chin, and stepped out her back door. The questions started as soon as the photographers saw her face. She wore oversized sunglasses and was sporting her A-game when it came to make-up and clothes. If she was going to hit the papers as the betrayed girlfriend, she wasn't going to be the devastated, couldn't-be-bothered-to-brush-her-hair-and-put-on-real-pants victim.

She waited for Sean to leave first. Russ and Leo arrived with two vans. They and Sean and Marcus darted in and out of the vehicles until the paparazzi were sufficiently confused. Sean made his getaway, leaving her with a parking lot full of vultures who wanted to see and pick apart her broken body.

They wouldn't get the chance. Besides, she had cried herself out in the shower. She trusted Sean. She did. In all her relationships, she had never gone out with a guy who'd cheated on her. Not once. There was the one jerk who called her from a bar and left her a voicemail telling her he was done with her working twenty-four hours a day and he was taking another woman home with him, but at least he'd dumped her first. Caitlin was ninety-nine percent sure Sean was telling the truth about Megan.

It didn't make the stories any easier to hear. And they were everywhere. On the television, on the radio, online. Caitlin lost track of how many people had sent her links to the stories. She didn't try to count the comments, whether they were supportive or gleeful about her situation.

But she couldn't have stayed in the shower forever. She was a professional actress and it was time to put her skills to the test. She could do this. Caitlin had spent extra time on her ponytail, making sure it was positioned for maximum bounce, and pulled out her waterproof mascara which needed the extra-strength make-up remover. Just in case.

She answered three texts before she headed out early to the studio. It would be easier to hide there. One to Sean to tell him she and Leo were leaving. She answered Ashleigh and Sydney's queries, which were both variations of "I heard. Want company?" Fortunately both her friends were self-employed and could give themselves the morning off. Caitlin sent back "thanks, but no thanks." She was good for now.

Caitlin was diligent as she made her commute. The

last thing she needed was to be involved in a car accident. The security guards at the gate looked twice at her, then let her pass without comment. She snuck into her trailer without running into anybody—it was early, even for her—but her solitude didn't last long.

"No comment," Caitlin yelled at her door.

"It's Jess. Open up." The pretty blonde actress didn't stop talking once Caitlin did as she was told. She simply brushed her aside on her way into the trailer. "You would not believe how exhausting bruised ribs are. Everything is attached to your ribs, did you know that? I'm going crazy. And my cats! I swear they're trying to kill me. You'd think they'd stay away after the first ten times I cursed at them, no, they're still playing slalom with my feet." She collapsed on the nearest chair. "If you were sitting here, too bad."

"I can move. You're here early. Do you want a coffee?" Caitlin snagged her coffee from beside the chair and burrowed under the blanket she had on the sofa.

Another knock prevented Jessica from answering. "God, yes. That'll be Layla. Be a sweetie and get her inside before too many people see her?"

"What's up?" Caitlin asked her guests.

"We're here for moral support. Jessica and I have both been caught in manufactured scandals. Do you remember my phantom baby? It took six months and copious staged photo ops in very tight clothes to go away," Layla said.

Caitlin remembered that story. It came out right about the same time Layla and Russ got serious.

"Everybody and their brother knows about my ex-husband getting, how can I put it, caught with his pants down during that website hack. Good times," Jessica said, sarcasm dripping from every word.

Oh, yes. Last year the number of broken marriages across the country spiked after a website designed for people who wanted extra-marital encounters was hacked. Jessica's husband at the time had been one of the more high-profile users who had been exposed. Caitlin never heard the details, but with the speed Jessica had filed and been granted her divorce, Caitlin assumed it had the potential to be very nasty.

She appreciated the support, but it wasn't the same thing. "I was sorry to hear about that. It's not the same. Sean didn't cheat on me. Megan isn't pregnant either," Caitlin said.

"Unfortunately for you, it really doesn't matter. People are going to believe the headlines. They want to believe the headlines. You've got to brace—and brace hard—for the fallout," Jessica said. The blonde was always smiling, no matter how quiet she was. It was wrong to see her serious.

"You're doing it right, though. You look great. Never let them see you sweat," Layla advised.

She wasn't going to whine. After a decade of wanting fame, she wasn't going to start bitching about the downside of it, not on her first time on the ride. Caitlin did allow herself one tiny complaint. "This really sucks."

Jessica offered her a toast with the coffee cup Caitlin handed her. "Welcome to Hollywood."

"Or shark week. Really, it's the same thing," Layla added. Caitlin had to laugh at the truth of the statement.

"What's Sean's next move?" Jessica asked.

Caitlin shrugged. "A denial, I guess. There's not a lot he can do beyond request a paternity test." She had no experience with stuff like this. She assumed Megan would have to agree to at least a pregnancy test if she was going public with the accusation Sean was her baby daddy.

"Are you going to stick it out with him?" Layla asked.

"Yes. He didn't do anything wrong." Her voice sounded sure. Perhaps she was a better actress than she suspected. Because believing Sean when he said he didn't touch Megan didn't stop the stabbing pain to her self-esteem every time she heard someone mention her dating a cheater, or her helpless anger that she couldn't say anything in her own defense.

"Don't change your mind halfway through," Layla advised. "Your relationship won't survive if you do."

Caitlin knew what kind of woman Megan was; she'd seen it firsthand. If it was he said/she said...Caitlin chose to believe Sean. He said he hadn't touched her, and Caitlin knew him well enough to tell when he was lying. He wasn't. "I'll stick," Caitlin promised.

Chapter 18

SEAN'S California King was much too big for one person. The knowledge he didn't have to be sleeping alone made his bed seem even colder. Caitlin asked if it would be better if she stayed with him for the night or if she should go back to her own apartment. He told her go.

He was an idiot.

History said if a man was accused of cheating and his woman stood by him, it blew over faster and created doubt about the accuser. He understood that; it made sense. But if Caitlin stood by him, she'd be covered in as much shit as he was. He wanted to protect her as much as possible.

Clark's statement to the press on his behalf was basic, but pointedly clear. No, Sean wasn't the father of Megan Unger's baby, and no, he couldn't be, since he hadn't been in a relationship with her in almost a year. The one thing Clark couldn't do was make them believe it. It was a better story if Megan's accusations were true.

It wasn't over. Not by a long shot. This was the initial volley; Megan had something else planned. He knew by her radio silence. On the upside, it would be pointless for her to try to kill him one week if she were going to file a paternity suit the next. Which meant Shannon Tolliver was now the number one suspect when it came to his car accident.

While he was at Clark's office, his agent had dropped a bomb about how many fan letters and packages Shannon had sent to him, which included locks

of her hair, a notarized blood test to show she was clean
of STDs, and a wedding ring engraved with their initials.
Clark had forwarded everything to Detective Brownlee.
The cops were tearing her life apart looking for the pick-
up that hit him.

Sean was not impressed when his phone woke him
before the sun rose after a restless night. He didn't need
the ringtone to tell him who it was. Only Clark would call
this early, and it wouldn't be with good news. "Hi, Clark.
What's up?" Sean asked.

"You said you didn't fuck her."

"I didn't."

"She has pictures."

"She can't have. If she does, they're from last
summer and I didn't know anything about them."
Dammit, he had no interest in making a sex tape. It
sounded like fun in theory, but they were dangerous as
hell in practice. He was never willing to risk it.

"She has photos of you with your hands on her
shoulders and her tongue down your throat. They're
definitely recent," Clark said. "It looks like—"

"A hotel corridor."

Goddamnconnivingbitchfacedwhore. He knew it had
been a set-up. He hadn't realized there were witnesses
with cameras. "She's using it for leverage, right?" Please
let that be it. If those got out, Caitlin would never forgive
him.

"No."

"Send them to me," Sean ordered. Maybe they
weren't that bad.

His phone pinged with a stream of incoming texts.
Shit! They weren't blurry security footage stills. His face
was fully in focus while Megan Frenched-kissed him.
None of the four shots showed him pushing her aside.

They were all from the first few seconds of the kiss when he still thought he was kissing Caitlin and was happy for the surprise. He scrolled through them again and his stomach flipped over.

Sean wheeled to throw his phone against the wall to destroy the devastating images. He fired it into his pillows instead. He couldn't destroy what might be his sole working link to Caitlin.

"Find out what Megan wants," Sean ordered.

It was early. If Sean was getting calls, Caitlin was getting calls. Her phone rang three times, and Sean could picture her staring at the screen, debating on whether or not she should bother to talk to him.

Caitlin took the call, and for a fraction of a second, he thought he might have woken her. Then he heard her icy, one-word greeting. "Sean."

"We need to talk. Can I come over?"

She didn't say a word.

"It's not what it looks like. I don't want to do this over the phone. Please, can I see you?" he begged.

"Not here. This is going to make my place a circus. I'm going to have a hard enough time getting away without you being here. I'll meet you at your trailer. In an hour."

This was not how Sean wanted to do it. He'd be better off meeting her at her apartment. It was more private and there were less people who could overhear their fight. And there would be fighting. It also gave him the edge of her not being able to leave since it was her place. She'd have to force him out, so the longer he could stall, the more chance he'd have of making her see the pictures didn't truly tell the story. At his trailer, they'd have to keep it quiet and she could walk out on him any time she wanted.

Sean couldn't let her walk. If he didn't talk to her, he wouldn't have a chance to stop her. "Okay."

The drive was hell. The roads were unusually clear, but every minute took a lifetime. Sean had taken another look at the pictures before he got into his rental SUV. For a kiss that had lasted a few seconds, the photographer must have been on standby. They were too clear to be using video stills.

Video. Holy shit, he might have a shot at proving Megan had blindsided him. He called Clark to see if the hotel had a security camera in the corridor. Clark was promising to look into it when Sean arrived at the studio.

Caitlin wasn't there. It didn't mean anything. He was right on time. She could have been caught in traffic. Or she got held up leaving her apartment. She was delayed, not standing him up.

He repeated that to himself for ten minutes while he paced in his confining trailer. Caitlin's truck drove by his window and she appeared at his door soon after.

"Did you see the pictures?" He asked. Silence greeted him. He took it as a yes. "Nothing happened."

"You said you didn't touch her," Caitlin finally said.

He had said that. "It's not what it looks like. I thought she was you."

Caitlin called the photo up on her phone. "Five-feet-nothing, red hair, big bust, all-gold outfit. Yeah, we were practically twins with my black hair, extra eight inches and turquoise dress. I can see how you got confused." What made his bad word choice even worse was her calm, quiet rebuttal while she smiled at him. If he didn't know her as well as he did, he would have believed it.

"We were at the Giving Back dinner and I couldn't find you. A hand grabbed me from behind and pulled me into a back corridor. I thought you were having a little fun and wanted to tease me with a hot kiss and make me wait for the rest of it. When I felt hands on me, I closed my eyes and went for it. I knew something was wrong almost right away and I got rid of her. The kiss was it. I swear." It sounded more sordid than it was, but he couldn't find the words to explain away an accidental grope session.

She wasn't speaking again. Emotions danced across her face so quickly he couldn't catch them all. Hope and disappointment seemed to appear the most often. "I swear, Caitlin. There's just you. I did not have sex with Megan in any way, shape or form. I love you." There was nothing he could give her to reassure her except words. He didn't know if they'd be enough.

Caitlin took a steadying breath, and another. She was working up to say something. Sean was willing to give her the time she needed, provided the words she chose weren't "good" and "bye." Before she said anything, they were interrupted by a knock at his trailer door.

"It is too fucking dark out for this shit," Martine said when she entered. Even at the early hour, the blonde was immaculately dressed and primped. The fire in her eye destroyed any image of her usual calm demeanor. "Tell me you two can work together."

* * * *

Caitlin woke to Ashleigh's pre-dawn knock on her door, and the certainty she'd felt the night before fractured into a million little pieces.

"Honey, I am so sorry," was all Ashleigh said when she handed Caitlin her tablet. There were four different tabs open and they all showed the same four-photo spread of Megan in her slutty, crimson dress, and Sean in his tuxedo, the pair joined at the mouth. She knew exactly when and where the pictures had been taken. Hell, she'd fixed Sean's tie after Megan had mauled it.

"The lying motherfucker!" Caitlin wanted to cry. Her eyes burned with tears but her shock and anger wouldn't let her. What she wanted more was to fight. "Didn't touch her, my ass," she growled.

Then Sean called, wanting to talk to her in person, and Caitlin agreed they needed to talk. Ashleigh shook her head at Caitlin's half of the conversation. When she hung up, Ash tried to talk her out of it. Caitlin would not be swayed. She was going to meet with him, but she'd be damned if she let him charm his way out of this. She deserved to have this fight face to face. He owed her that.

She took extra care in getting ready. If yesterday had been horrible, today was going to be a hundred times worse. She beat the vultures by seconds. She pulled into the street just as a photographer she recognized parked across the street.

Sean sounded sincere, and the stress on his face looked genuine as he apologized. His explanation even made sense for what had happened. But he kissed Megan and lied about it. He didn't have a real excuse for the lie. Before she could question him further, they had an audience. Martine gave her a once over and nodded approvingly.

"It is too fucking dark out for this shit. Tell me you two can work together," Martine ordered.

"We can work together." Caitlin answered for them both. She'd be damned if she was going to lose her job over this situation. Sean nodded in agreement.

"You do know about the pictures, right?" Martine asked her.

"Yes."

"It would help if you two are seen out in public together."

"We were just discussing that," Sean said. He looked at Caitlin, but he didn't elaborate. She didn't either.

"The sooner the better," Martine advised. "What do I need to know here?"

"Megan jumped me in the corridor and kissed me. I scraped her off. She propositioned me. I turned her down. I got out of there. Nothing else happened," Sean said.

Megan had propositioned him? Yet another thing he hadn't mentioned. Caitlin winced when her nail cut deeply into the palm of her hand. Sean seemed to be leaving all kinds of things out of his conversations with her.

"The studio is not getting involved in this. My job is to make sure you two don't tank the show's popularity. Make sure this doesn't mess us up." Martine stalked over to Sean. "Fix this fast," she said. "And for fuck's sake, clean yourself up. Shave. Fresh clothes. Pressed shirt. Slacks or good jeans. Haircut. Don't look like you're hiding. That's the fastest way to admit guilt."

"I'll be photo-ready the next time I step out the door," Sean promised.

"Good. If something else happens, it would be a nice change to hear it from you and not the press. Now I have to go find coffee."

Martine vanished as quickly as she arrived, leaving Sean and Caitlin staring at her. Sean had an "I love you" look on his face. It turned her stomach. Caitlin needed to clear the air before he got into that again.

"What else does 'I didn't touch her' and 'nothing happened' cover?" she asked. "Because so far we have unmentioned tonsil hockey and fellatio offers. How about hand jobs? Do those not count either? What about sexting? If I exchange naked pictures with some guy, am I required to mention it or can I write it off as 'nothing happened'?"

An instant flush covered Sean's face. The vein in his temple began to throb. Caitlin didn't care. She wasn't the one obfuscating about old lovers. "You're saying you sent skin shots to Greg?" he said, one word at a time.

"What? No! You don't get to be mad. How the fuck did this end up you accusing me of infidelity? I'm not the one who's hiding shit," she yelled. Caitlin was tired of being the calm one, the understanding girlfriend. She deserved answers and she was getting them. Now.

"I wasn't hiding things," Sean yelled back.

"No? Because you didn't mention getting cornered until it came out in Megan's press release. You didn't mention kissing her until the photos were leaked. You didn't mention her inviting you to pick up where you left off until you were talking to Martine. How can I not wonder what else you didn't mention?" Caitlin asked.

She didn't realize she was crying until Sean's rough hand brushed her cheek and his thumb wiped away the tear that escaped the corner of her eye. "I swear to you, there's nothing else. Not with Megan, not with anybody. I thought I was protecting you by not telling you. I am very sorry for hurting you. I've never had to protect anybody before. I fucked up, Caitlin. I swear, there is nothing else. Nothing."

"How am I supposed to trust that?" She could close her eyes and take a leap of faith, but the last time she'd done that she'd ended up in her current predicament. A second bad jump could kill her.

"Because I would do absolutely anything for you. I'll do whatever it takes to prove it."

"Then stop lying. And omitting. And protecting. Because you're doing more damage to us than Megan is."

"Anything, baby. I love you." He couldn't stop

himself. He had to make sure she wasn't going to run. Sean reached for her. Once she was in his arms, he buried his face in her hair. "If I forget to tell you something, it's because I've forgotten, not because I'm hiding it. I'll bust my balls to make sure it doesn't happen again. Okay?"

Caitlin nodded, words beyond her.

"To be clear, now that I've got you in my arms and I'm not about to let you leave me, we're good, right? We're solid."

She nodded again. She didn't tell Sean he was on his last chance. She didn't have to. He knew he'd pushed her as far as she was willing to go. Even trust had a cut-off point. But until she reached that, if he was fighting for her, she could return the favor.

Chapter 19

AS his razor scraped the last of the stubble from his face, Sean felt truly clean for the first time in days. He ran his comb through his hair again, taking care not to muss the sharp part on the side. He couldn't do much about the circles under his eyes. Perhaps he'd visit the make-up trailer later. For now, he had sunglasses.

He was very lucky. Caitlin could have walked. She could have spoken out and destroyed his reputation, lack of evidence be damned. She could have done anything and, after his stupidity, he would have had to take it. She'd decided to stay. He would spend the rest of his life making sure she didn't regret it. Even if that meant putting himself in the public eye and taking the hits so she didn't have to. It was the least he could do to protect her.

Caitlin went to her own trailer to wait for him to get ready. They decided a brief appearance at the studio's canteen to get the ball rolling. It was public, but not a complete free-for-all. He and Caitlin ignored the subtle and not-so-subtle phones and cameras pointed their way while they ate a very early breakfast. He didn't expect the good stuff to happen on their way back to their soundstage.

Two buildings down from them, on the other side of the SWAT Boyz soundstage, was home to Georgetown Performing Arts, a teen drama set in a Fame-like high school for artists and performers. Caitlin had told him the dance scenes were below average. They stepped aside to let a golf cart by, and were knocked into the wall when a side door flew open and two kids shot out.

"I'm not the one screwing up the steps," the shorter, female one said.

"It's not my fault you can't keep up," the stretched, skinny male one shouted back.

"Tours are starting for the day. You're in public. Act like it," Sean said.

That shut them up for a moment. "Great, we've got Sir Cheats-a-lot and his pussy of the month giving us advice now," the boy said.

If pressed, Sean would say he had no idea how the kid managed to trip over his foot and go sprawling on the pavement. If the boy didn't smarten up, it would happen again. The poor kid also bounced off the exterior wall when Sean helped him up. "Apologize. Now."

"Sorry," the teen muttered.

"You're Anna Pickering and Daniel Cope. I'm Caitlin Kelly. Can we help?" Caitlin asked.

"I don't think so," Anna said. The tiny African-American dancer shrugged. "It's a dance problem. Daniel's problem, not mine," she specified.

"I minored in dance, and I work with Ashleigh Jessup. Try me," Caitlin said.

Sean had no idea where Caitlin was going with this, so he kept his mouth shut. He smiled to himself when he recognized the problem Anna described. It was one his mother had to train him out of when he first discovered girls liked boys who could dance. "She's right, it's your fault," Caitlin said to Daniel.

"It's not my fault. I'm not getting the steps wrong. I'm one of Sandrine Gold's top students," the black-haired boy protested.

"And let me guess, every partner Sandrine ever gave

you was maybe a few inches shorter than you. You're not doing them wrong. You're doing them wrong for this partner," Caitlin explained. "You're more than a foot taller than Anna is. Your steps are too big for her to match. Cut your distance in half."

She grabbed Sean's hand and wormed her way into his arms. If they had been in the safety of his living room, she'd be flush against him, pressing her breasts into his chest, and his hand would be on her ass, not her waist. But, as he told the kid, they were in public. "Stop me if I'm wrong, but I'm betting right now, you guys are having problems something like this," she said to Daniel.

She whispered instructions to Sean on how she needed him to dance badly on purpose. Caitlin did her best to keep up with his long legs. She only made it a dozen steps before she tripped. Sean pulled her close to keep her from falling, and swung her into a deep dip before pulling her up. "Were we close?" he asked.

"Pretty much," Daniel said grudgingly. "So how do I fix it?"

"My mom made me tie a string around my knees to force me to take smaller steps. Mostly you have to listen to your partner," Sean said. He steadied Caitlin on her feet and they danced again. Sean's steps were only half as long as they had been, and Caitlin didn't have to stretch to keep up. They made the short circuit around the teens and back to their starting point.

"Keep in mind, smaller steps also let you move faster, if you're ever doing a quick number," Caitlin added. "You can't only learn the steps. You have to learn how to do them with each new partner."

"Aren't you two broken up?" Anna asked. She immediately covered her mouth. It looked like she was trying to stuff the words back in.

"No, we're not." Sean said.

"We are, however, going to be late," Caitlin added before Sean could continue his intended lecture. "Do you have this now?" she asked Daniel.

"I think so. Thanks. Sorry about the…" Daniel stammered.

"Don't do it again and we'll call it even," Caitlin said. "Remember what we showed you. I hope it helps."

Sean held her hand for the rest of the walk back. He couldn't figure out why she inserted herself into the kids' conversation. Or why she offered to help. She wasn't the type to force herself into a situation. They were in the parking lot when his phone began to ping. After he read the first message, he understood.

"You set me up," he said after the truth of the situation hit him.

*

"I did not set you up. You were there with me helping!" Caitlin nudged him with her shoulder. It sucked they couldn't issue a statement saying Megan Unger was a lying skank who was out for revenge after being dumped. Since that option was off the table, they had to get creative. Being photographed having breakfast together was one thing.

Smiling while dancing in each other's arms made a much deeper statement. Caitlin hadn't asked the studio's photographer Benny Duarte to come around the corner with his camera right before Sean dipped her. She certainly couldn't be held responsible if the tourists in the golf cart took pictures and shared them on their social media accounts. Nor could she stop Anna and Daniel from telling everybody on Georgetown Performing Arts she and Sean were still a couple, because God knew teenagers weren't going to sit on fresh gossip. All she'd done was dance with her boyfriend. "You're the one who made me laugh while we were dancing."

"I pay Clark a lot of money for his advice. He specifically told me not to comment on Megan," Sean said.

"We didn't say a word about her. Her name never came up. You know it. You should also know sometimes a girl has to make a statement without making a statement. So I did. Are you seriously pissed at me?" she asked. She hoped not. If he was, the other idea she had was really going to piss him off.

"No." He stopped in the middle of the street and kissed her to prove it. Not a naughty kiss, but he made his point. When the tip of his tongue touched hers, Caitlin was painfully reminded one night away from him was too long.

Their thirty good minutes came to a screeching halt when a mob was waiting for them at Sean's trailer. "Oh, God, now what?" Caitlin muttered under her breath. Sean's grip tightened around her fingers but he didn't falter. "What's up?" he asked Chris.

"Don't panic," Chris said.

"That's not a good way to start," Caitlin commented. She looked at the other concerned faces in the group. Layla. Nick. Glinda. Mike. Jessica and Jason. "We're not panicking. Why should we not panic?" she asked, panicking just a little.

"This week's scripts are out," Chris said. "Psyche dies."

"Well, fuck." She wasn't joking. Everybody laughed anyway. That's all she needed. There had always been a chance she wouldn't survive the season, being one of the few mortals on the show, but she thought the fan love and resulting publicity Psyche and Eros brought to the show would be incentive for them to renew her contract.

"Didn't we tell you not to panic? It's okay," Layla said.

"How can it be okay? I'm dead!"

Sean got it first. He wasn't just a pretty face. "Tell me the writers are following the original mythology."

"They are," Jessica said. "But you might be dead for an episode or two before Zeus gets around to reviving you."

"Are we sure they are going to bring me back?" Caitlin asked.

Jason rubbed the back of his neck. "I may have cornered a few writers and taken a peek at the whiteboard for upcoming episodes. Yeah, we're sure."

She'd take Jason's assurances for now. Caitlin excused herself to go to her trailer and grab what she needed to bring to the table-read, where they'd go over the new script. This newest development had her thinking. She almost had a plan. All she needed now was the time difference between Los Angeles and Sydney, Australia.

She couldn't make the call she wanted to until later in the afternoon. It was hard to find time between work and friends popping by to make sure she was okay. Finally, she locked the doors, and waited for the video link at the other end to open.

"Hi, Jared. Thanks for taking the time today," Caitlin said in greeting.

A slight lag between the video and audio gave the reporter a stop-motion look. "It's my pleasure. I was surprised to get your message."

"I wanted to say thank you for the great piece you wrote about me. I know it was about the show so I appreciate your Charlie Oscar Echo mention."

"Any news on your next album?" Jared Parker asked.

"I think the band is issuing a press release in the next two or three weeks." And if they weren't, Caitlin would write it herself. They might not have a replacement for her by then, but it would be public knowledge they were looking. Which reminded her, she had a couple names she wanted to throw Peter's way.

"I don't suppose you want to comment on Sean's paternity suit," Jared said.

"His press release stands. He isn't the father. Their relationship ended last summer. I have no comment on the matter."

"Any thoughts on who the baby daddy is?"

Caitlin smiled at him. "I'm certainly not saying you should look for a star in the East."

The reporter laughed with her. "Funny. Those pictures say differently," he pressed.

"Come on, Jared. You were at the same party we were. We both watched Sean get jumped by a fan in the main ballroom. Twice. It's funny that there were, what, maybe a dozen blurry shots between both extended encounters with her, and Megan got four perfectly framed shots taken in a five second period. I wonder where those pictures came from anyway?" she wondered aloud. She didn't say it looked suspiciously like a set-up because she thought the reporter was smart enough to fill in the blanks himself. "I'm going to be very relieved when she finally issues her retraction."

"Do you remember when I said you were doing well for a beginner stepping into the spotlight? I take it back. You're doing extremely well for an experienced veteran," Jared said.

"Thank you. I try hard. And I'm a fast learner."

"So, Miss It Girl, what's next for you? Those

dancing shots are something else. Any more moves like that in the works?"

"Not that I know of, but you may want to check back with me in a couple months," Caitlin said. She actually saw the reporter's ears perk up at her comment. She glanced at the list she'd taped to the wall behind her tablet, mentally noting she'd commented on everything she wanted to and hadn't said anything she shouldn't.

"News on the band definitely coming, news on dancing or maybe a new role potentially coming. Any news on Olympus?" he asked.

"Now, Jared, that's cheating. I'm having lots of fun, though. Every episode this season is unbelievable. You won't believe what you're seeing." She needed to end the call before she screwed it up. Her luck wasn't going to hold forever. "It was great talking to you again. I hope you look up Charlie the next time you're in LA. I'll be sure to have tickets waiting if they're in town," she said.

"Sounds great. Thanks, Caitlin."

The screen went dark, and Caitlin shut her tablet off to be sure the connection was broken. She'd walked right up to the line and tap-danced on it, but she hadn't stepped over it. She hadn't given Jared anything he could use right away. He may not be able to use anything she gave him.

But he might.

Chapter 20

"CAITLIN! What did you do?" Clark was screaming at him. His phone was screaming at him. Martine was screaming at him. He wanted to share the wealth.

"Nothing?" He almost believed her. There was something in her eye though.

"Caitlin?"

"I just got here. I haven't had time to do anything."

This was true. He'd arrived at his place long before Caitlin, who'd been pulled into a disagreement between the wardrobe designer and the seamstress on set. When she'd finally arrived, a tornado of leaves and dirt came through the door with her as the windstorm outside strengthened.

"So you have no idea how the hotel's security footage got leaked to Hollywood 24/7?"

Her eyes lit up like a kid at Christmas, but there was surprise there too. "That is fabulous! Please tell me it's as damning as you told me it was." She watched open-mouthed as he played a clip showing a blind clinch, a hot kiss, and him freaking out when he realized who it was. "Damn," she said when it was over. "I had nothing to do with this. I swear. I wish I'd thought of it though. Are you sure it wasn't Clark?"

His agent had been his first call. Sean didn't have time to ask a single question because Clark thought he was the leak. He didn't hesitate to defend Caitlin, willing to protect her if she had snapped from the stress. He was relieved when her reaction was too shocked and gleeful to be anything but honest. "Megan's cornered now. She either has to retract her claim now, or go ahead with the paternity testing and get crucified in the press for falsely accusing me later. Either way, she's screwed."

"I guess that will depend on whether she has the money to keep paying her lawyer," Caitlin said.

She was right. Megan's lawyer was probably banking on a portion of the settlement she'd no doubt demand. A third of nothing was a good reason to dump a losing horse. Whoever the video-leaker was, Sean owed them huge.

As for his own response, it was too early to celebrate. However, if he made a reservation for a romantic restaurant for next week, the timing would probably be perfect. While he was deciding if he wanted to go steak or something fancier that Caitlin might like, his phone rang. "Hi, Leo." Since Caitlin was back staying with him, Leo Vukovich had deemed one man guarding the house was sufficient.

"You had somebody on your property. They jumped the fence. I'm in pursuit, but that means you're down to your house's electronic system. Make sure it's on," Leo said. Sean heard him panting and footfalls slapping the pavement.

"Got it." Sean ended the call and turned to Caitlin. "I'm kicking you out for the night."

"I didn't do anything!"

She opened her mouth to protest again. He shut her up the most fun way he knew how. Angry Caitlin kisses were the best, along with sleepy, good morning kisses, take your pants off now kisses, and pretty much any other kind of kiss when it came to her. He pulled her close; his arms wrapped around her waist, until he drew her to her toes and forced her to lean against him for support. He nipped at her bottom lip to stop her from talking, then did it again because he liked the whimper she made. His tongue darted into the heat of her mouth. He could never get enough of the taste of her. Why the hell was he sending her away?

A branch slapped the living room window, breaking Sean's concentration. He looked twice to make sure he didn't see a face through the glass, and set Caitlin back on her feet. "You really have to go. Somebody tried to get to the house. Leo went after them. Leo's brother knows what he's doing. He says to lock this place down. If there's a possibility of them coming back, I don't want you here. It's not safe."

"Okay. Grab your overnight bag. Let's get you in my truck."

"I'm staying."

"Well, that's stupid. If it's too dangerous for me to be here, what makes it any safer for you?" Caitlin argued.

Usually he loved it when she never gave him an inch. Not this time. "Leo will be back in a couple minutes. It's not like I'll be alone. But a bodyguard can only guard one body at a time. Nothing has happened at your place. I'd rather you be there with Marcus across the hall." His lips found the spot below her ear which always made her shiver. "Please," Sean said.

"You are such a cheater," Caitlin groaned. "Fine. I'll go. This time. If I have to come back here with my 9mm to save your ass, I will not be amused."

"Text me when you get home," he ordered. Sean kissed her again, and it was next to impossible to let her go. The fear of her being here if the intruder came back got him moving. Once Caitlin cleared the gate at the front of the property, Sean closed and locked every door and window on the main floor.

The alarm beeped when Leo opened the gate and jogged up the driveway to the house. He shook his head before Sean could ask. "No, I didn't catch her. I did identify her though. Shannon Tolliver strikes again."

Sean had felt a tiny bit of sympathy when the woman first hit his radar. He'd been star-struck himself when he was in university. He, however, had managed not to track the actresses back to their homes and try to force his way into their houses. Leo took a moment to double-check the same entry points Sean had inspected before they decided to move to the kitchen.

A thump on the second floor and a cold breeze down the staircase froze Sean in his tracks. He hadn't opened any windows or doors upstairs. Leo held a finger to his lips. He pointed at Sean's study on the main floor; a room with a solid wood door, interior lock, and a single window. Sean nodded and pulled out his phone. He'd pressed the 9 and first 1 by the time he closed the door behind him.

Home invasions were pretty much guaranteed to have a high priority. Add in his fame and the fact he had stalker complaints on file, and somebody had recently tried to kill him, and the dispatcher promised a quick response. Sean disconnected in time to hear a couple thuds, some cursing, and a crash that sounded suspiciously like the mirror in the hall hitting the hardwood floor, before Leo gave him the all-clear.

The stacked brunette in zip cuffs sitting on the floor at the base of the stairs stared at him, a look of innocence and confusion on her face. "Why did you send your attack dog after me, Eros? Don't you remember? You invited me over. I was planning a romantic evening for the two of us and he ruined it. Why didn't you leave my name at the gate? I should have been able to come in the regular way. Are you ashamed of me?"

A pissed-off six-foot-five redhead and a calmer but armed black man should have broken through her delusion. Sean would have been scared if he were in her position. She hadn't blinked when Leo had put the zip-cuffs on her. "Sean, don't engage with her. I've already called the cops," Leo said.

"Why are you denying what we could be? I can't believe you went and got serious with Psyche. She's nobody. She's so self-absorbed she won't have any time for you. She won't support you like I can, Eros," Shannon pleaded.

She was completely locked into the fantasy of him being a Greek god, she couldn't even use his name. Sean almost felt bad for her. She needed help. Help far away from him. "One question while we're waiting. Why did you destroy my car door?"

"That was an accident, Eros. I wanted to key Psyche's car. When I crouched down, my backpack squished against your car. Then I stood up to take it off and the zipper rubbed again. And then some guy hit an alarm and it startled me. I fell against your door. And then I scraped it again getting back up. And then I had to run because I didn't want to get in trouble for trying to vandalize Psyche's car," she said without stopping once to breathe.

His baby, damaged by accident. It was a tragedy of Greek proportions.

"And my house?" he asked.

"You invited another woman into our sacred home. I was upset."

"This is my house. You were never welcome here." His harsh words made her gasp, but he turned his back and strode outside to wait for the cops before she spewed some other whacked-out explanation that would piss him off further.

When the police arrived, Sean confirmed he was going to press charges. All the charges they could come up with. Vandalism, trespassing, breaking and entering. He didn't say a word to Shannon as she was taken away in handcuffs.

It was too late for Caitlin to come back for the night, but he did call to tell her Shannon had been caught and it was over.

Caitlin didn't pick up.

Neither did Marcus.

* * * *

Caitlin knew why Sean had sent her home. It was cute in an overprotective, he-man way. It would have been cuter if he'd recognized she could take care of herself. She reminded herself of his position and decided not to push the issue; he was stressed out enough as it was. This was a minor concession on her part. She could hold her tongue for one night.

The parking stalls at the back of her apartment were empty. Ashleigh appeared to be spending the night at Nick's. Marcus's car wasn't there either. Sean told her before she left his house that her bodyguard would meet her at her place. She'd obviously beat him there.

Perfect. She could get in some bass practice.

She took a sip of green tea and got the lyrics sheets in front of her organized. She may be on her way out of the band when it came to performing, but that didn't mean she couldn't keep a hand in when it came to song writing.

Marcus knocked on her door a few minutes later to let her know he'd arrived. Caitlin absently responded, her mind on the music in front of her. The crash of metal on metal that immediately followed fully captured her attention.

"What the hell?"

Marcus turned away from the window at the end of the hall. "Somebody in a white pick-up rammed your white pick-up, babe. I'm going to go check it out," he said.

"Don't go out there! Have you never seen a horror movie? That's how the bad guys get you. Call the cops," Caitlin shouted.

He didn't listen. Marcus was halfway to the main floor when the entire building heaved.

It wasn't an earthquake. That felt different. The Duncan Building had withstood the tremor that had taken out Jessica without as much as a cracked wall. This had been an impact of some kind. Caitlin heard the unmistakable explosion of a pane of glass shattering.

No more than a second later the sound of grinding metal and falling bricks screeched through the ventilation ducts, as well as the roar of a revving engine. Her brain slowly filtered the new information. Somebody had rammed into the building.

Caitlin forced herself to stop at the door. If it were a legitimate accident, the driver would have to wait thirty seconds while she got her gun, called Marcus's security main office, and dialed 9-1-1.

The bottom of the staircase was gone. Marcus lay in a pile of bricks, metal bars, and linoleum tiles. The white truck he mentioned seconds before was half buried as well. Caitlin jumped from the last intact stair to the hood of the truck. Without warning, it revved its engine and shot backward. Caitlin tumbled to the floor beside Marcus, her gun going flying and sliding down a crack into the rubble. "Marky-Mark! Are you okay? Marcus, wake up!"

Her bodyguard didn't move. He wasn't leaking red from anywhere Caitlin could see. Internal injuries were another matter entirely. She didn't move him, just in case.

She couldn't have if she wanted to, though. The pick-up screeched to a halt a few yards away, a plume of steam and black, oily smoke escaping from under the hood. The driver's door flew open and a familiar redhead jumped out.

Armed.

It took Caitlin's option to run out of play. "This is stupid, Megan. The police are already on their way." Her heart was pounding out of her chest. She climbed to her feet, moving away from Marcus in case Megan's aim was bad. It took everything she had to keep her knees from shaking. She fought the urge hard; she refused to show weakness.

Megan didn't look good. Caitlin wasn't referring to her broken nose, or the friction-burned skin on her face where the airbag had most likely made contact. It was the way the barrel revolver in Megan's hand waggled around as Megan stumbled around. The redhead held it in a one-handed grip, trying to stem the blood flowing from her nose with the other. With the barrel occasionally pointing her way, Caitlin figured the best way not to get shot was to stand still and let Megan do the moving.

"Hands up, bitch," Megan ordered. Caitlin did exactly as she was told. She needed to buy time.

"Look what you did to my face! You are fucking up my life," Megan shouted. "I've been working my ass off to get Sean jealous enough to commit and you appear out of nowhere. I should be living large already. Nice clothes, nice car, nice parties. Then you had to come along, and now that I really need a good guy to step up, you've hooked the only available one I know."

So she really was pregnant. "Shooting me isn't going to make Sean marry you."

"It could. It might be the leverage I need. You were jealous and asked me to come to your apartment to bribe me to go away. You went nuts and shot at me. I had to defend myself."

The plan was as stupid as Megan was. "I hear sirens, Megan. You have time to run."

A cruiser that had silently rolled up the alley loosed a loud whoop over its speaker. Caitlin hadn't taken her eyes off of Megan's gun since it came into view. When she saw Megan's hand jerk, Caitlin hit the ground and wrapped her arms around her head. The explosive noise of a gunshot echoed in the lane.

"Freeze!"

"Drop the gun!"

Caitlin heard the clatter of metal hitting pavement, followed by, "She was trying to kill me, officers! It's her. Arrest her!" Megan's squeals got higher as her protests got louder.

"Miss, are you all right?" a male voice asked.

A hand touched her shoulder and Caitlin jumped. She lifted her cheek off the concrete enough to take in the leather shoes and uniform slacks beside her. She lifted herself a little higher to see the dark face of the man crouched beside her. "Miss, are you okay? Did she hit you?"

"Not with the gun. I don't think."

The nice officer helped her to her feet while his partner executed an unfriendly weapon search on the now-prone Megan. Her own pat-down was much gentler. "She's clean," her cop said.

"What happened here?" his partner asked once Megan was in cuffs.

"Marcus—Marcus Bolling, my bodyguard—is inside. He needs an ambulance. Megan rammed the stairwell when he was on it. I couldn't get him to wake up. He's not bleeding that I could tell. He's—"

Megan cut her off, screaming an expletive-filled rant, which alternated between giving the story she'd told Caitlin she was going to tell, and cursing out the police for being incompetent. Megan had just gotten to the part where she claimed Caitlin had fired at her first when an ambulance arrived, followed by an unmarked police car pulling up alongside, its lights flashing through the front grill. A familiar SUV pulled up after that. She spotted Sean and Leo's faces through the windshield.

"I'm fine!" Caitlin braced for the rib-cracking squeeze she knew Sean was about to deliver. "I fell down the stairs. Well, what's left of them. I'm not shot. Megan missed."

"She tried to shoot you?" Sean's tone dropped below arctic. His focus changed in a heartbeat. Suddenly Caitlin was the one holding on to him.

"She's under arrest. If you do anything to her now, you get arrested and she walks. I know you're angry. Don't do let her win. Don't let her take you from me after all of this," she whispered in his ear.

"Can you get her out of here?" Sean asked the cop who'd helped her up, tilting his head at Megan. His ex-girlfriend had begun ranting again, this time about how Sean was ignoring his duties as a father. "Like, now?"

The police loaded Megan into the original cruiser and the noise level on the scene dropped by half. They were well into the wee hours by the time Caitlin finished giving her preliminary statement. Leo agreed to stay with the building until it could be repaired the next day. With Sean's place a crime scene, her place a destroyed crime scene, and dawn approaching, they decided to save themselves some time and crash in Sean's dressing room trailer.

Caitlin struggled to pull away from Sean and give him some space. She was suffocating him, she knew. As the night progressed, she'd burrowed deeper into Sean while she spoke to the various officers and detectives, first for emotional and then physical support as the seriousness of the situation hit her. She'd nearly been shot. Megan could have killed her. All because she wanted Sean as her sugar daddy. "I don't want your money," Caitlin suddenly said to Sean.

He sat on the narrow bed to look down at her. "I didn't think you did."

"I'm not with you because you're famous either," she added.

"I know, Cait. Where is this coming from?" He ran her ponytail through his hand in a soothing rhythm.

She closed her eyes at the simple comfort. Her eyes burned with unshed tears of relief. "I don't ever want you to think I was using you for your fame."

Sean laughed. Belly-laughed. "Honey, I hate to break it to you. In another year you're going to be more famous than I am. Don't get me wrong, I'm doing okay, and I'll work my ass off to keep things okay, but you have more drive and bigger ambitions than I do. I want to rule television. You want to rule the world. When you do, I promise not to use you for your fame either. Unless it's a part I desperately want. Or you have a chance at courtside seats."

"You're an idiot and I love you."

"I love you too. Go to sleep. Tomorrow is going to

be hell," he said.

"You're going to be here tomorrow, right?"

"Of course."

Caitlin shut her eyes. "Then it's not hell."

Chapter 21

SEAN needed to do something nice for Suzan Platt, the show's make-up artist. She made him look human and camera-ready after three hours of sleep. It was magic.

When he and Caitlin had arrived at the studio in the dead of night, the security guards blinked, but let them through. Sean desperately wanted to spend the next week holding Caitlin in his arms to assure himself she was safe and in one piece. He'd done everything right and taken the threats against him seriously, yet he'd still underestimated his stalker. Stalkers. Plural. Nobody saw that one coming. Marcus hospitalized and Caitlin shot at. Shot at. Fuck.

He'd been waiting for the situation to hit and freak her out. By the time they'd crawled into the bed, small and crappy as it was, she was already asleep, completely exhausted from the physical and emotional crashes she'd had in the last few hours. Sean slept lightly, keeping an eye out for signs of Caitlin slipping into another nightmare. However, she didn't as much as roll over. The only noise she made was when he shifted his arm off her waist. He put it back immediately.

When his alarm went off, set for the last possible minute, Caitlin's eyes popped open. She was fully awake, without even the scent of coffee. "This isn't going to last long. I'll be running on fumes by lunch," she said. Her voice was odd. Her inflections lacked the emotion that should be there. It didn't ring true.

"Babe? What are you thinking?" he asked. If last

night had been too much for her, Sean didn't know what he'd do. Maybe finish the season and kidnap Caitlin and get her out of the city. Keep her in bed until she agreed they deserved another chance together. If they made it through the disaster that was currently his life, they could survive anything.

"I'm waiting for the other shoe to drop," she said.

"What other shoe? You don't think I have a third stalker, do you?" he asked. "Or are you expecting other bad news?" She'd had her own share of shit since they'd begun filming the fourth season.

"I don't know. Maybe I've been waiting for so long for your stalker to be caught, that my body still thinks it needs to be on guard. Do you think it's over?"

"It's over. You can relax. I think you and I will have clear sailing from here on out. We have three episodes left. What do you think of getting away for a while after we're done?" He could take her home to Wyoming. Introduce her to his family. Have Leo and his company rewire his entire property again while they were gone. Maybe move Caitlin in at the same time. Sean had a feeling Caitlin would need the extra security sooner rather than later. He'd read her movie script. If he had any instincts at all, it was going to hit huge. As much as she liked her apartment, she'd have to give it up sooner rather than later, for safety's sake.

"I'll try."

She relaxed a little after that, and more once they got a call from Leo telling them Marcus had been released from the hospital.

As if he weren't raw enough, today was the day they were filming Psyche's death scene. Caitlin was set to die in his arms from a gaping spear wound in her chest. He didn't know how he was going to find a balance between shutting down to prevent a flashback of last night's alternate real-life ending, and allowing enough emotion through for his performance to be real.

* * * *

Sean was on the other side of the battlegrounds during the fight scenes. He didn't want to watch Caitlin get skewered over and over again. He stayed away while they dabbed her with the cherry-colored fake blood. When he got the call for "Action," he sprinted across the backlot outdoor set, jumping over the bodies of fallen soldiers of the various gods' armies. He looked at his grievously injured girlfriend, who was sprawled across a pile of rubble, and hit his mark, barely.

"Psyche? You'll be fine," Sean said as he brushed Caitlin's sticky hair off her face.

"I love you, Eros," Caitlin said, her teeth stained with red syrup.

"I'll fix this," he promised.

"I love you."

"We've been through too much for me to lose you now." Sean was peripherally aware of the camera lens zooming in on them, but he didn't look away from Caitlin's face. She didn't respond. Didn't move. Her expression didn't go lax; the only difference was the light had gone out of her eyes. The change was startling. It took him a moment to realize she wasn't breathing either. "No, no, wake up!" He shook her slightly, and Caitlin's head lolled in the crook of his arm. "I love you." She didn't blink. "I love you!"

Caitlin was dead-weight in his arms. The edge of panic that he'd felt the night before flooded him again. "I'll bring you back. I swear. After I do, I'll kill them all."

"Cut!" the director yelled from behind the cameras.

Caitlin drew in a massive breath. Her eyes refocused on Sean. "Nailed it!" she crowed.

"Fuck, that was awful," he said. Sean couldn't help himself. He lifted her and kissed her, in front of the crew and everybody. Despite the pale make-up she wore, she was warm and soft and responsive. Sean kissed her thoroughly, until the cheers from the crew distracted him. "Do me a favor? Get rid of your cherry-flavored lip gloss for a while. I don't want to be reminded of you looking like this." He could go the rest of his life without seeing a blood-spattered Caitlin, on set or off.

The director walked over to them, the once-dead soldiers moving out of his way. "We aren't doing another take. You two were perfect. Sean, I don't know how you managed to tremble like that when you were holding Caitlin, but damn, it looks fantastic. And, Caitlin, wow. Just, wow. This might be Emmy role stuff."

"I have room on my shelves for an Emmy," Caitlin said. Then she cackled. "As if I'd have a shot. You are too cute."

Sean didn't say a word.

* * * *

Caitlin's fingers ached as they gripped the neck of her favorite bass guitar. This was her farewell performance with Charlie Oscar Echo. Her movie shoot started the next week and things got progressively crazier after that. The last two episodes closed the season with a bang. Her character was resurrected by Zeus and was now immortal, and the battle ended with a split in the Greek pantheon, which now divided the mortal world. The critics were raving. There were rumors—multiple rumors—about the show getting Emmy nominations. Most of those rumors had her name attached.

But announcements weren't for another couple

weeks. Her break from acting had been long enough to do a short round of LA clubs with the band while they finished interviewing replacement bass players. The unanimous choice had been Georgia Keene, who'd defected in a nasty split from Neverland, the long-time opening act for Mastersounds. Tonight was Georgia's introduction to the world as a member of Charlie before they started a multi-state tour as the second opening act for one of the biggest bands in the country. They were on their way. Although Caitlin swore she was okay with leaving, her breath caught every time she thought of it.

Caitlin stole a glance at Sean, who was off to the side of the stage. He'd made all of her shows except one when he'd been out of town at a fan convention. As the band eased into their final song of their third set, Caitlin grabbed her microphone.

"Hey there, Diamond Room. You know, this is the first place in LA I played with Charlie Oscar Echo. It seems fitting I'm ending things here. So, since this is my last official song, I want to send it out to my guy over there. I'm getting better with the words."

She sang Break for the last time. It was the album's title track for a reason. It was a heart-wrenching ballad about refusing to break under the pressures of the world, and standing by your one true love. It wasn't a bad way to go out.

Two encores later, Caitlin packed away her guitar. She'd play with the guys again although it would never be the same. Sean joined them for a drink after the bar closed, and she had another one after that. She eventually had to say good bye.

"Jesus, Cait-girl, you're not dying. You already have tickets to our show next week. Turn off the waterworks, woman!" Bobby complained after she gave him his third hug.

Greg ducked behind Georgia. "Bye, Caitlin. Have a good night. Sean, get her out of here before she goes around again," he said.

Sean laughed at him. "Fine, I'll take pity on you guys. Come on, Cait, let's go home."

"Your bed is going to feel like heaven," she said as she settled into the passenger seat of Sean's new Maserati. Her mind was spinning, but her body was exhausted.

"Whose bed?" Sean asked.

She'd forgotten. "Our bed." She was still getting used to living in Sean's house. He'd invited her to move in with him permanently while her apartment building was being repaired. She had turned him down flat. She wasn't ready for that step. It took a few days for her to realize he moved in some of her stuff "to make her feel at home" because the contractors were taking longer than expected. She found she liked living there, although she wasn't comfortable calling it "her" place yet.

"Get used to it. The movers are bringing the rest of your furniture this week."

"My IKEA specials are not going to work with your designer furniture in your designer house," Caitlin protested.

"It'll fit because you fit. I love you, Caitlin. I love having you in my bed and in my house and in my life."

What else could she say to that?

"I love you too. Take me home."

The End

About Elle Rush

Elle Rush is a contemporary romance author from Winnipeg, Manitoba, Canada. When she's not travelling, she's hard at work writing books which are set all over the world. From Hollywood to the house next door, her heroes will make you sigh and her heroines will make you laugh out loud.

Elle has a degree in Spanish and French, barely passed German, and is learning Italian and Filipino. She flunked poetry in every language she ever studied. She also has mild addictions to tea, cookbooks and HGTV.

For the latest updates on Elle's books, please check out her website and sign up for her free newsletter at www.ellerush.com/newsletter, or follow her on Facebook or Twitter.

Check out the other stories in the
Hollywood to Olympus series

SCREEN IDOL
DRAMA QUEEN
LEADING MAN
IT GIRL
ACTION HERO (coming 2017)

River City Heroes series
PURSUIT
ENTRAP (coming 2016)

www.ingramcontent.com/pod-product-compliance
Lightning Source LLC
Chambersburg PA
CBHW070849120626
46556CB00002B/932